All Things Heal In Time

The Never Miss a Sunset Pioneer Family Series

Previously published as
Call Her Blessed

Jeanette Gilge

LIFEJOURNEY
BOOKS

David C. Cook Publishing Co.
Elgin, Illinois • Weston, Ontario

LifeJourney Books is an imprint of David C. Cook Publishing Co.

David C. Cook Publishing Co., Elgin, Illinois 60120
David C. Cook Publishing Co., Weston, Ontario

ALL THINGS HEAL IN TIME (formerly *Call Her Blessed*)
© 1988 by Gilge, Jeanette

Edited by LoraBeth Norton
Illustration by Ben Wohlberg
Cover Design by Dawn Lauck

First Printing, 1988
Printed in the United States of America
92 91 90 89 88 87 5 4 3 2 1

Gilge, Jeanette.
 All things heal in time.

 Summary: Emma's constant struggle to keep her family fed and thriving in their rural northern Wisconsin community is complicated when the death of her daughter Emmie leaves her to raise her infant granddaughter.
  1. Country life--Fiction. 2. Christian life--Fiction
 I. Title.
 PZ7.G395A1 1988   [Fic]   88-3580
 ISBN 1-55513-474-2

Contents

THE VERLAGER FAMILY TREE
(Emma and Al)

Children	Spouse	Grandchildren
Albert	Maime	Paul, Arthur, Ruby
Fred	Helen	Kermit, Everett
Ellen (Ella)	Henry	Carl, Edward, Harvey, Harold, Myrtle, Grace, Jim
George	Sadie	Dorothy, Norma, Glen, Ardis, Owen, Betty, George, Jr., Bunetta, Gardia
Leonard	Nora	Elaine, Goldie, Shirley Emma, Joy Ann, Len, Jr.
Minnie	Nels	Amy, George, Rose, John
Edward (Eddie)	Connie	Allison, Shirley, Maybelle, Marylou, Richard, Edward
	Peggy	Rosemary, Gordon, Kathleen, Frank, Ruth
John	Esther	Jean
Gertrude (Gertie)	Joe	Clyde, Earl, Don
Roy	Helen	Ronald, Marilyn
Emma (Emmie)	Ed	Jeanie
Carl	Olga	Albert
Henry (Hank, Henny, Lefty)		

One

Starting Over

A tiny baby crying . . . crying.

Emma pulled the comforter up over her chilly shoulder *Why doesn't someone take care if it?* she wondered as her thoughts floated between layers of unconsciousness. She had never allowed her babies to cry like that. So long ago—all those babies.

Poor little thing. Maybe she should get up and take care of it. No. She'd had twenty years of crying babies. Thirteen of them, to be exact. It was someone else's turn.

Sleep closed over her thoughts again, but the crying continued. Poor baby! She'd better see—

Emma heaved her body out of bed and opened her eyes, and the moonlit room snapped into focus. Baby Jean! Emmie's baby—her baby now. How could she have forgotten, even in sleep?

She scooped up the tiny bundle, stuck her feet into slippers, and padded toward the kitchen.

"There, there, Liebchen," she crooned as she lit the little kerosene burner and poured milk into a blue and white speckled saucepan. The baby screamed in her ear as she stuck the funnel into the narrow bottle neck and filled it.

Wrong! So wrong! This baby should be warm

and cozy at its young mother's breast. A sob, always close these days, erupted as Emma thought of that lovely young body, lying lifeless up on the hill near Papa's.

When the baby's cries gave way to the sounds of contented sucking, she leaned her head against the high-backed rocker.

The clock struck three.

Three more hours of sleep—if the baby slept. She was so tired. . . .

She felt the baby slipping from her arms and jerked. That hazy dream. . . . If only it had been someone else's baby she'd heard. If only she were still keeping house for Roy and Carl and Hank, free to help with the milking and feed the chickens and garden and knit and talk on the phone and sleep all night through.

"Oh, Father," she whispered. "I don't understand how you could let Emmie die and leave this little one. And now I should start all over again with another baby? I'll be seventy-two when she graduates from high school!"

She eased the baby into her bassinette and crept into bed. "I could cry for a week," she told herself, "but I don't have time. I'm so behind with work. Tomorrow I'll wash those lamp chimneys and bake bread and scrub the floors and get started on the garden. And the baby will cry and cry."

She was about to cry herself when she remembered: Gertie was coming!

She smiled, sighed, and slept.

When Emma heard Roy and Carl go out to do chores, she hauled herself out of bed. Thank goodness, she hadn't had to call them since the baby came.

But fourteen-year-old Hank—Henny, she called him—that boy was another story! She decided to dress first and then go up and wake him instead of tapping on the ceiling with the broom handle. Might wake the baby.

Too late. The baby's little arms were waving, and she started to cry.

Emma hurried to the kitchen, lit the kerosene stove, and built a wood fire while the milk heated.

"Wouldn't you know it!" she muttered as the kerosene flame flickered and went out. "Empty."

Must tell Roy to buy more kerosene when he goes to Ogema after Gertie, she told herself as she lifted the smelly can and filled the stove.

By the time she had it filled and lighted, the baby was screaming. No need to go upstairs to wake Henny. She tapped three sharp taps on the ceiling, and his heel tapped three back.

When she had filled the bottle, she quickly put more wood on the fire and settled down in the rocker with the baby.

No Henny.

Screaming baby in one arm, broom in the other, Emma tapped three I-mean-business taps. Henny answered with two I'm-coming thumps.

Eye on the clock, she eased herself back into the rocker. As the baby's cries ceased, she realized that the tension inside her had already begun to tighten like a huge clock spring—and the day had barely begun.

Ten minutes passed. No Henny. Roy and Carl were none too patient with him at his best. If he'd only hurry! Why did he always have to drag behind?

Ear tuned for the creak of his bed, she waited as the baby burped and dozed.

I'd better get him up now, she decided, *before the baby goes back to sleep*. Emma headed for the stairs.

Halfway through the dining room, she heard him coming, sighed, and sat down again. She'd try to be patient.

As he laced his boots, tousled hair falling over his eyes, she said, "Henny, it would help so much if you'd get up when you hear the boys get up."

"Don't hear 'em."

"Well, then, get up as soon as I call you or rap."

"Yeah, yeah."

"Hurry up and help the boys now, and after breakfast you stay with the baby while I feed the chickens."

"Aw, Ma! All she does is bawl, and I don't know what to do with her."

"All right! All right! Just get going now!"

He slammed the door, the baby's little hands flew up, and Emma's tension spring tightened another notch.

"Oh, Father," she whispered. "Why? Please help him do what he should."

With the baby asleep again, Emma hurried to the kitchen and set the big, black frying pan on the front stove lid. She spooned lard into it and reached for the kettle of boiled potatoes she always peeled the night before. Empty.

"I know I planned to boil them. . . . How could I forget?" she muttered. They'd just have to eat more bread, and she'd fry a few more eggs.

Emma ground coffee, wishing she had thought to do it while the baby was awake, filled the pot, and hadn't even finished setting the table when Carl came in with the milk.

"When's that kid gonna start gettin' up and helpin' us? He only milked one cow this morning!"

Emma felt the spring tighten another notch. "It's hard, Carl. I don't want to wake the baby. . . ."

"That's all I hear around here—don't wake the baby!" He slammed the door before she could answer.

She turned and reached into the bread box. "Oh, no!" she wailed, holding a stub of a loaf. She'd have to fry pancakes.

The boys were washed and at the table before the first pan full was done. Roy shook his fork at Hank. "You clean the barn this morning. Carl's going to be out in the field, and I'm going after Gertie."

"But I gotta feed chickens," Hank protested.

Carl tilted his chair back and let out a hoot. "Big job!"

Roy scowled at both of them. "You clean the horse barn, too! When I was fourteen. . . . "

Hank waved his hand. "Oh, I know, I know. You ran the whole place single-handed."

"Boys! That's enough. Oh, for goodness sake, there's the baby again, and I have to fry pancakes."

Carl unwound his long legs from his chair, headed for the bedroom, and came back awkwardly patting the baby, who sounded like she might stop crying.

Emma gave Roy the first pancakes.

Hank growled.

"Henny, you hold your horses. Roy's got to get going—Gert'll be waiting. And you too," she told Buckley, the little white terrier who sat quivering in anticipation of left-overs a discrete distance from the table. "Roy, you sure the roads are all right?"

Roy nodded. "I talked to the mailman yesterday. Some spots planked yet, but I'll be careful. He said the sink holes are the worst since he's been on the route."

After the boys had eaten and gone out, Emma poured a cup of coffee, speared a cold pancake, and tossed the rest to Buckley.

Quiet. Blissful quiet. She wanted to sip her coffee and think over the past weeks—maybe even cry and get rid of that ache in her throat.—but there was no time.

"Emmie is gone!" she told herself, for the hundredth time. "And the baby . . . the baby is here. For good."

She washed the last bite of pancake down with coffee and set the dishes together to make room for mixing bread. She hoped to get the kitchen floor scrubbed before Gertie came, but all she had done was wash the dishes and feed and bathe the baby when she heard the car drive up.

Little Clyde burst in the door, followed by Gertie carrying chubby little Earl.

Emma patted Gertie's fresh young cheek, hugged little Clyde, and reached for Earl. "My land! He weighs a ton, compared to Jeanie. And look at him smile!"

Gertie was already holding Jeanie. "Oh, Ma, she's so tiny! So thin! Is she still throwing up so much? Have you weighed her? And her cheeks are so rough and red!"

Emma sagged into the rocker. "Well, she isn't throwing up quite as much—not like she did in the hospital. They'd prop up a bottle with a big hole in the nipple, and she'd gulp it down, throw it up, and cry another four hours."

"You think Emmie could hear her?"

Emma took off little Earl's sweater and shrugged. "I don't know. The times I was there, they had her anywhere there was an empty bed. Couldn't put her in the nursery, 'cause she wasn't born there."

Gertie shook her head. "Emmie was so happy—so proud of her." She blinked back tears. "Ma, if you want to work in the garden, I'll take over in here."

Emma nodded. "I'd like to get started out there. Carl helped me scratch in a few peas last week, but it's high time to get the root crops in." She put on her straw hat, sticking a metal knitting needle through the hat and her pug as she told Gertie what she planned to cook for dinner.

As she hoed and planted, the tension inside her unwound little by little. It was good to know Gertie was with the baby. Those boys just didn't know what to do when she cried.

Emma straightened up and rubbed her tired back. The leaves almost full-grown now. Lilacs budding. Surely the violets were in bloom down by the river, but there was no time to pick them for the graves for Decoration Day this year. She'd put the pink geranium on Emmie's grave and transplant some creeping myrtle from Papa's and plant a red carnation on Papa's as she had done the last five years. Five years! And now he had his little Emmie with him.

She tore open an envelope of carrot seeds. Such a short while, it seemed, since last spring when Emmie was still teaching in Kennan—all excited about teaching closer to home the following fall.

She was in love with Ed, yes, but at nineteen not ready to get married. But they had. Quickly. Quietly.

"The baby will be born the middle of April," Emmie had said. "Oh, Mama, it was just that one time. . . ." She had cried and cried.

Emmie had taught until Christmas, and then they had moved her ivory bedroom set and cedar chest to Phillips, to Ed's family's farm house where his brother Charles and his wife, Sodonia, lived.

Emmie had been happy to be in the same house with Sodonia, her friend and former schoolmate, and didn't mind the tiny rooms. In summer they'd buy a house in town near Ed's garage.

But the baby had come March 31 in the midst of a blizzard, and four days later they had loaded Emmie into the baggage car of the train on a stretcher. The fever she developed the second day was raging by the time she was admitted to Ashland General.

Emma started when Hank slammed the garden gate. "Gertie says dinner's ready."

The fragrance of fresh-baked bread greeted Emma as she came inside. She pulled the knitting needle out of her hat and hung it up, as little Clyde clamored at her feet, pointing to her head. She picked him up. "What is it, honey? What do you want to tell Grammy?"

Gertie came over, potato masher in hand. "Tell Mommy. What are you trying to say?"

Clyde examined Emma's head with a pudgy finger.

"Oh, Ma! He's looking for the hole in your head! He thinks you stuck the knitting needle through your head!"

The women laughed, and Clyde's little lip trembled.

Emma hugged him close and smiled, "Oh, sweetheart, we weren't laughing at you." She took the needle and stuck it through her pug. "See! Here's where it goes!"

The boys trooped in, and Roy grinned. "Sure good to hear someone laughing around here again."

"You know," Emma said as she cleared the table after dinner, "this was the first meal I haven't had to force down."

Gertie laughed. "Must have been my cooking. Couldn't have been the exercise."

Emma reached for her straw hat.

"Ma, you look awfully tired," Gertie said. "Why don't you take a little nap before you go back out?"

"Well, I suppose I could—for a little while. Not long, though. I want to hoe the cabbage patch and set out these plants."

It was two-thirty when Emma's sleep-creased face appeared at the kitchen doorway.

Gertie looked up from cleaning lamps and smiled. "Now, don't fuss, Ma. You needed that sleep."

Emma sat down heavily. "I thought it was morning and I'd slept the whole night."

Gertie pulled the coffee pot over to the front stove lid. "I'm just about done here, and then we can have a cup of coffee."

"But there wasn't enough kerosene. I forgot to tell Roy to get some in town."

"I found a little more in the barn," Gertie said, replacing the last chimney. "There's enough in them for tonight."

Emma poured steaming hot coffee while Gertie put away the lamps. Jeanie's bottle was warming in the tea kettle. "Look who was waking up," Gertie said, holding baby Jeanie's rough little cheek close to hers. "She's been a good girl today."

Emma sighed. "I hope she sleeps tonight."

Gertie shook a few drops of milk on her wrist and sat down. "Bless her little heart, she's starved! Oh, I didn't get to tell you—I went to see Minnie Sunday."

"How is she?"

"Miserable. Sure hope that baby isn't late. She wanted to hear all about everything. You know how hard it is for us to believe Emmie's gone, and we saw her laid out and went to the funeral and everything.

"I told her how pretty Emmie looked in that pink chiffon dress and about the pink rose buds Ed had me pin on the puffs of the casket lining and how she looked like she was just sleeping and how beautifully Roger Evans sang. She cried a lot, but she needed to get it out."

Emma nodded. "Ella and I were talking the other day about how hard it would be for Minnie, because she couldn't be there." Emma bit her lip. "The worst part is waking up in the morning. For just a moment, it's so good, and then I remember. . . . It was so different when Papa died. He was sick so long and suffered so."

"I don't think I grieved for Papa till months later," Gertie agreed. "After I forgot about the suffering a little."

"I had a letter from Ed, poor man. He says if it wasn't for the baby, he wouldn't want to live."

"Do you think he'll take her, if he gets married again?"

"No. He promised Emmie he never would. She wanted me to raise her."

Gertie caught her breath. "Then she really did know. She didn't let on, the last time I saw her. When I came, she was coughing hard, and the nurse asked me to wait outside in the hall.

"When I went in, she was propped up, smiling and said, 'Gee, Gert, that dress looks good on you!' And later she talked about making a little dress for Jeanie out of her lavendar voile with the white embroidery, because it was tearing under the arms." Gertie blinked hard.

"The day I took the baby home—that was only five days before Emmie died—one of the nurses told me they'd hear her crying at night. But all she said to me was, 'You took good care of all of us, and I know you'll take good care of her.' I left her with the baby a few minutes before we left. . . ." Emma's voice broke. "I think I knew then, but I didn't want to believe it."

Gertie put the baby down and gathered Emma in her arms. "Oh, Ma. I try not to be mad at God. . . ."

"I know, I know. I don't understand . . . but I know I love God, and I know He loves us."

Two

Buckley

"I wouldn't feel so tired," Emma told herself as she put potatoes on to fry the next morning, "if I weren't so used to sleeping straight through." She hadn't tried to count how many times she'd been up with the baby in the night. "Feel eighty-five instead of fifty-five."

She peered out at the gray eastern sky through the pantry window, remembering that the diaper pile was getting mighty low. She'd have to dry them on the back porch if it didn't clear up.

She took the baby's bottle and put it back in the tea kettle, grateful for every quiet moment.

It wouldn't be quiet long. She could hear little Clyde bouncing on the bed upstairs. Just thinking of Gertie going home today brought tears to her eyes. She'd miss her companionship as much as her help with the work—though the help was certainly appreciated.

She put on a smile when Gertie and the children came downstairs. "You go up and wake Uncle Henny," she told Clyde. "Tell him to get up right now!"

Sunbeams had gilded the porch posts by the time breakfast was over. It would be a beautiful wash day after all, the women decided. They recruited Henny to carry pail after pail of water from the pump by the kitchen door to fill the big copper boiler and two wash tubs.

While the water heated, Gertie bathed the babies.

"Should we weigh Jean, Ma?"

"Oh, yes! I've been wanting to do that." She lugged the heavy old scale in from the milk separator room and lined the scoop with a blanket.

While Gertie's hand hovered over the baby's tummy, Emma moved the weight until it balanced. "Seven pounds, fifteen ounces," she proclaimed. "Almost eight pounds."

Gertie picked up the crying baby, blanket and all. "That's only seven ounces more than when she was born, and she's almost two months old."

"She was only seven pounds when I brought her home three weeks ago. Do you think something's wrong with her?"

Gertie frowned. "I don't know. Why don't we see how she does in another week and then, if she isn't gaining faster, maybe you should take her to Doctor McKinnon. He might be able to give you something for that rash, too."

Emma nodded. "I'll try to get her to eat more."

After the diapers and tiny clothes had been washed, boiled, and rinsed, Gertie and Emma worked together hanging them.

Emma shook out a diaper and gave it a smart snap. "Never thought these old lines would be drying diapers again."

After a few minutes Gertie went to check on the little ones. Emma thought she should work in the garden while Gertie was here, but what she really wanted to do was sleep and sleep. She wouldn't think about it. When she came in, Gertie was gathering Clyde and Earl's toys and clothes together. Roy had said he would take her home after dinner.

Emma started to tell Gertie how good it had been to have her home, but she began to cry in the middle of the sentence.

Gertie slipped her arm around mama's shoulders, and Emma dried her eyes with her apron. "Silly goose! I didn't think I was going to cry. Just hate to have you leave, but I know you have a lot of work to do, too."

"Nonsense! I can stay another day. Joe won't be home until Friday. We'll work on our garden Saturday.

"Oh, Gertie, would you? You just don't know. . . ." She started to cry again.

"I'll stay under one condition."

"What's that?"

Gertie wagged her finger under Emma's nose. "That you take a nap after dinner."

Emma sat down in the rocker and heaved a sigh. "I won't even argue."

They were feeding the babies later that afternoon when Gertie said, "Are you planning to take her out Decoration Day? It's next week you know."

Emma shook her head. "I don't think so. She cries so much I probably wouldn't hear the speaker anyway. And even if that rash is gone, I don't think it would be good for her."

Gertie sighed. "I wish you could come. It's the one time of the year the whole community gets together and you see old friends."

"Guess I'd just as soon not see them right now. Maybe by next year it won't hurt so much to talk about Emmie."

"I dread talking with people, too, even though they mean well. But I do look forward to seeing the rest of the family. I talked to Mamie the other day, and she said the boys have new white sailor suits and Ruby has a new blue dress for Decoration Day."

Emma laughed. "She'll be scrubbing grass stains off

Art's the next day for sure, but Paul's won't have a spot. Like night and day, those two boys."

"Wait till you see all those little cousins," Gertie said to Clyde as he snuggled up against her.

Emma and Gertie reviewed the names of twenty-one cousins, while Clyde listened in wide-eyed wonder.

"I can hardly keep track!" Gertie said with a laugh. "What will we do when John and Roy and Carl and Hank have kids?"

Clyde squirmed down and ran off, with Buckley at his heels. A moment later he ran back, crying and pointing at the dog, who cowered under the dining room table.

Gertie examined Clyde. "I don't see any sign of a bite or even a scratch."

Emma stalked into the dining room, crouched down, and shook her finger in the little dog's face. "What's the matter with you! Did you growl at him? Outside with you now! Get!"

Tail between his legs, Buckley scooted out the door.

"I don't know what's ailin' that dog. Could he be jealous of the baby?"

"Maybe. He's been the whole cheese around here for a long while." Gertie chuckled. "He should know he's the only dog that was ever allowed in this house."

Emma smiled. "I'd always said I'd never have a dog in the house, but I couldn't stand to see him shiver out there. When we ordered him, we didn't realize that he'd have such short fur. He has been a good dog— except for the time I found him in the pantry."

"On the fly paper?"

Emma laughed. "I can still see him! I had just put down a new sheet of Tangle-foot, and didn't he sit on it!"

"I wish I'd seen him."

"I tried not to laugh while I scolded him, but he looked so guilty—like a little boy caught with his hand in the cookie jar." Emma frowned. "I hope there isn't something wrong with him. I'd miss that little fellow."

"Maybe he just needs more attention," Gertie suggested, putting Earl down on a comforter on the floor.

The day Gertie went home, Emma put the baby down on the comforter. Buckley came out from his favorite spot under the table and curled up on a corner.

"Good," Emma said to herself. "Maybe he won't be so jealous if he can share her comforter."

At noon Carl brought in the mail and sat down to read the *Youth's Companion*. A few minutes later he yelled to Emma, who was in the pantry.

"Mama, what's the matter with Buckley? He's almost shakin' his fur off."

Emma came to see. "Well . . . I never saw him do that. Isn't cold today. Wonder if something scared him."

Carl cradled Buckley in his arms. "What's the matter, old boy? Does something hurt?"

Buckley licked Carl's face.

"Whew! Does his breath stink!"

Emma leaned closer, then made a face. "Ugh! I suppose his teeth are bad. He's getting old, you know. Wash up now; dinner's ready."

Emma put the baby on her comforter in the dining room while they ate dinner in the kitchen. Buckley seemed fine, curled up on a corner once more.

"What we need," Roy said, reaching for the potato bowl, "is a farm dog—a collie we can train to chase cows for us. Ran my feet off after those dumb heifers."

A good idea, Emma thought later, as she lowered a stack of plates into the dishpan. *Anything to make the boy's work easier.*

The baby's sharp cry startled her, and she ran to the dining room. Buckley had backed off his corner of the comforter, where the baby had rolled. His fur stood up, and his teeth were bared.

Emma snatched the baby and glowered at him. "Why, you cross old dog, you! Don't you dare hurt this baby. Get outside now."

She held the door open and watched him slink outside. "Little dog," she said with a sigh, "I'm afraid your days are numbered."

Three

Gustie's Rebuke

When Decoration Day dawned cloudless, Emma almost changed her mind about going to the community gathering at the cemetery. But when the baby screamed all the while she was being bathed, and napped only minutes at a time, Emma knew she would stay home.

She would have a little holiday, anyway, because she wouldn't have to cook. The ladies of the Norwegian Lutheran church always served dinner, and the boys would enjoy eating there. They'd be eating ice cream cones sold by the American Legion, too.

After they were gone, Emma swept the kitchen and fixed the baby's milk for the day. Then she put on a sweater and took her knitting out to the porch swing. By now the program at Wilson School would be over, and they'd be marching to the cemetery. The firing squad would fire a salute over the graves; little ones would hold their ears and babies would let out startled cries. There'd be tearful parents placing flags on sons' graves and, surely, prayers of thanks for others' safe return. Once they were home and safe, it was easy to forget to be thankful.

Emma stopped her work to thank God once

again for her Eddie's safe return. "Lord, I don't know what Eddie's doing today in Eu Galle, but no doubt he's thinking of his dead buddies and of those awful times. Father, please take those bad memories away, so they don't keep him from being the man you want him to be."

How they had tried to get Ed back before Papa died! The Red Cross had tried to help, but Eddie had come home on the very last troopship, and Papa had been gone six weeks. *Maybe God wanted to spare Eddie seeing Papa frail and weak.*

Emma shook herself back to the present. No use thinking about that now. She'd not waste this precious quiet time. It was good to sit still and rest.

Oh, dear! The baby already. She put down her knitting with a sigh and went to heat a bottle.

Emma put the little cap Emmie had crocheted on the baby, tying the pink ribbon under her chin. Then she wrapped her in a blanket and took her out to the swing. She tried to sing as she fed her, but every song she tried made her want to cry.

Right now people would be walking through the cemetery, admiring plants and flowers. The Verleger lot would look nice, with the pink geranium and the red carnation and the grass freshly cut. At least she had been able to get up there and help the other day.

Some folks would stop at Emmie's grave and say, "What a shame." or, "She was such a special girl."

Even before she was born, Emmie was special. Emma had hardly been able to believe she was really having another baby. Three years earlier, when she had had the stillborn baby and the infection, the doctor had said she would never have another child.

So Emmie had been especially precious. All the baby things had been given away, so Emmie had new ones. It had been a thrill to dress her in soft, new little saques.

. And now, this baby. So different. So difficult.

"Never had a baby who cried like this," she said to herself. "And this rash—I can never tell if it's better or worse. One day I think I should take her to the doctor, and the next day it looks better, so I wait again."

She'd better lay Jeanie down and get more knitting done. The boys had worn out so many socks last winter, she'd have to knit like everything to replace them.

No sooner had she come back out and sat down, than the baby cried again.

"What's the use?" Emma muttered as she tied the little cap back on and took the baby back outside.

She wanted to relax and enjoy looking up at the gleaming white clouds and the deep green of the pine and spruce trees against the blue sky, but her eyes kept straying to the dandelions along the driveway. She didn't dare look at the garden, where she knew weeds all but hid the vegetables.

She wished Ella and her family would stop on their way home, but it would be chore time and they'd have to get right home.

Wish I had one of those ice cream cones, she thought. *I'm as bad as the kids when it comes to ice cream.*

Emma was so absorbed in her own thoughts she wasn't aware of a car driving into the driveway until it sped past the end of the porch and on to the rear of the house. She had only a brief glimpse of the passengers—could it possibly be Gustie and one of her boys?

Emma hurried through the house to the back door. There was no one she'd rather see than her light-hearted sister. If anyone knew what Emma had been through, it was Gustie. Her home in Ashland had been their refuge those five weeks when they'd visited Emmie in the hospital. Driving over a hundred miles on muddy spring roads hadn't been easy.

Emma flung open the door. "Gustie! It is you! I'm so glad. Come in! Come in! Luke—bless you, boy. Did you have a good trip?"

After hugging Emma, Gustie shed her coat and reached for the baby. "Still a skinny little thing, aren't ya! Aw, never mind. Some day you'll be fat like your Aunt Gustie. How's she been, Emma?"

Emma shook her head. "She cries so much—and her skin . . ."

"Looks like eczema to me."

"Eczema?"

Gustie shrugged. "Don't know exactly what it is, but one of mine had it. The doctor gave me some salve to put on it, and it went away evenutally."

Sometime after two the next morning, Gustie came downstairs and held out her arms for the crying baby. "Let me take her. You go get some sleep."

"Oh, no! You go back to bed. I wouldn't sleep anyway."

"Try it," Gustie ordered, extracting the baby from Emma's arms.

And Emma did sleep—straight through till the boys got up.

As Gustie worked by her side the next day, Emma poured out her grief and frustration. The crying baby, Henny's rebelliousness, the never-ending work.

"Every now and then I see this—this picture in my mind's eye. Emmie walks in, all bright-eyed and strong, and says, 'Mama, I'll take her now.' "

Gustie, usually ready with a bright quip, didn't say a word.

"Why is taking care of this baby such a chore for me?" Emma asked her directly, after receiving no answer for a long while. "After thirteen babies, you'd think it would be easy."

"For one thing," Gustie answered, "you're forgetting that many of those babies were taken care of with the help of older children. Minnie and Gertie took care of Henny almost more than you did, after he was weaned."

Emma sighed. "That's another thing! I can't get used to those bottles. All that washing and boiling and mixing. And it takes her forever to eat, while I sit there looking at all I have to do."

"Prop the bottle up and go to work, then! She needs to be held, but not all the time!"

Again, that night, Gustie took her turn with the baby so Emma could sleep.

When it was time for them to leave, Gustie hugged Emma hard and long. At the doorway she turned and said, "Emma, I just don't know how you're going to do it—"

Emma nodded solemnly in agreement.

Then she finished, "—Love that baby and feel sorry for yourself at the same time." And she strode out to the car, leaving Emma open-mouthed.

Stunned, Emma turned her back. *Sorry for mysefl! I am not! All I did was tell her how things are!*

She got out the big aluminum bread-mixing pan and made a nest of flour. "Humph!" she muttered. "Easy for her to talk. She can go back to her nice, quiet house."

She added potato, water, shortening, salt, and the yeast she had set the night before, and stirred in the flour with a wooden spoon.

Indignation rose in her like bubbles in a pot of thick oatmeal. Spoiled. Pampered. That's what Gustie was! No chickens. No separator to wash. Just a cozy little house in town, with a bathroom. And how those boys catered to her! Hadn't she said that all she had to do was tell Willie what she wanted planted where, and it was done.

I can just see Henny doing that! And here I thought she'd understand!

Emma sifted flour over the spoon, rubbed off the soft dough, and began to knead the bread. She sniffed and wiped a tear from her cheek with her flour-sprinkled arm, ignoring the crying baby.

Oh, Gustie had been helpful, that she could say. But why not? It wasn't hard to help for a few hours or even days. . . .

At dinnertime, Carl took one look at her and said, "Ma, what's the matter with you?"

She pretended she hadn't heard him.

"One of you could hold that baby," she snapped as she dished up the food. She was aware that they exchanged glances and shrugged. Roy picked up little Jean.

After dinner she tried to lie down for a few minutes, but as soon as she did the baby started to fuss. "Oh, what's the use?" she grumbled. She picked her up and walked back and forth the length of the house.

Why? Why must it be this way? The phone rang. It was Mrs. Allen, a favorite neighbor.

"Emma! How are you?" she asked, but the baby began to cry before Emma could answer.

"Oh, dear! I hear the baby. I'll let you go. I just wanted to let you know that I feel so sorry for you. I don't know how I'd start all over again with a little one. Keep your chin up now!"

Emma thanked her and hung up, feeling justified.

She laid the baby down and let her cry while she put the bread in pans, but her jaws ached with tension and she felt trembly inside.

"I can't do it!" she sobbed as she covered the loaves with a clean dish towel. She sat down in the rocker, her apron over her face, and sobbed softly.

"Father, I'm so miserable! Help me!"

She thought again about Gustie's words: "I don't know how you're going to do it—love that baby and feel sorry for yourself at the same time."

Love at the same time as I feel sorry for myself. . . .

She dried her eyes and tiptoed to the bedroom where the baby was sleeping. She picked up her old, leather-bound Bible and turned to the slip of lined paper that marked that special spot in I Corinthians.

Lips moving, Emma read, "Charity suffereth long and is kind: Charity envieth not." *Oh, Lord, I do envy Gustie.*

She read on, and phrases jumped out at her. "Charity is not easily provoked . . . beareth all things, believeth all things, hopeth all things, endureth all things. . . .

She staggered back to the kitchen rocker. "Charity" was the same as love, she knew; Rev. Fischer had explained it to the ladies group one Sunday afternoon.

"Oh, Lord," she groaned. "I see that I can't do both at the same time. I've got to make up my mind. What will it be?"

She closed her eyes and words echoed in her head—beareth . . . endureth . . . is kind . . . suffereth long . . .

"All those ugly thoughts. I'm so ashamed. Forgive me. And help me. I want to love like that."

The baby started to cry again, but instead of the usual tight resentful feeling, there came caring warmth—like she used to feel with her own little helpless ones.

Emma rushed to Jeanie, picked her up, and crooned, "It's all right. It's all right. Grammy loves you."

One day the boys laughed at the baby and said she was "all mouth" when she yawned. Emma scolded them, and Roy said, "All right, Mother Hen, don't ruffle your feathers. We won't laugh at your chick."

Yes, Jeanie was beginning to feel like "hers."

Then one day, after her bottle, the baby smiled—a genuine I-know-you-smile. Emma hugged her close.

"Oh, you little sweetheart! It's so good to see you smile!"

Soon after that, she made another discovery: the baby didn't cry while the phonograph was playing. Emma only wished records were ten times longer. At mealtimes, when the baby was fussy, the boys took turns hopping up to change records.

"When we get some extra money," Emma said, as

they listened to "Where the Silvery Colorado Winds Its Way," "let's get a new record. I think I've heard them all a hundred times. Maybe we could get another hymn by Henry Burr."

Even the baby's rash didn't concern her as much, since Gustie had said it would go away—until Ed came one Sunday. Jeanie's little face was raw and rough and, though Ed tried to hide his distress, she saw tears in his eyes.

She tried to explain what Gustie had said, but it didn't sound convincing even to her.

"Maybe you should take her to Dr. McKinnon," Ed said, quickly adding, "but you do as you see fit."

Emma dabbed at the weepy spots that cracked when the baby cried or smiled and said she thought that was a good idea. She had never taken her children to the doctor—but this one was different.

Ed brought a crib with him that day. "She'll be able to look around and be more content," he said.

When it was set up, Emma folded a large sheet and tucked it around the mattress. She put the baby in it, and they said at the same time, "She looks so little!"

He brought a canvas swing to hang in the doorway, too, but the baby was so small Emma had to put a rolled-up blanket around her so she wouldn't fall over.

Tuesday it rained and Roy couldn't work outside. He suggested taking the baby to the doctor.

"Infantile eczema," Dr. McKinnon pronounced. "Usually lasts until they're done cutting teeth. Don't worry about it. It will go away."

"Will she have scars? Her cheeks often crack and bleed."

The doctor shook his head. "Never saw anyone become scarred. Try this in her milk instead of what you're using." He handed Emma a can of Melon's Food. "And here's some salve that might help a little."

When Emma phoned Ed that night, he sounded much relieved.

"It just isn't like raising one that's born to you," Emma said to Roy. "It's like working with someone always looking over your shoulder."

She longed to say more, but she couldn't expect a twenty-one-year-old to understand how it felt to be facing all those years of child-rearing while one's own strength gradually ebbed away.

As she undressed, her apprehension grew until it became cold fear. What if she didn't live till Jeanie could be on her own?

Far into the night, she tried to imagine little Jeanie in one after the other of her children's homes. Each time she simply didn't fit.

"Father," she pleaded, "please keep me strong and well until she doesn't need me anymore."

Four

Colonel

It was the last week of June when Gertie called. "Minnie had a little boy last night! His name is John. Everything's fine; Dr. McKinnon was there in plenty of time. "

Emma was glad for all the news. "And," she reported, "I weighed Jeanie yesterday morning: eight pounds, eight ounces! She's gaining!"

"The Melon's Food must agree with her."

"Doesn't seem to be helping her skin, though. I was hoping it would clear up. Oh, did I tell you about the trouble we're having with Buckley? He's having more of those shaking spells, and he's so snappy. I hate to get rid of him, but I'm afraid he might bite the baby. With those awful teeth of his, she could get blood poisoning."

Two days later, the baby and Buckley were sharing the comforter while Emma and the boys ate breakfast. Suddenly the baby screamed, and they all ran to see what had happened.

Buckley disappeared under the table, but there were indentations of his teeth on her little arm. The skin wasn't broken—Jeanie was more frightened than injured—but Emma's voice shook.

"That does it! I can't watch that dog all the time, and we can't risk having her bitten. Anyway, he could be sick. He's got to be shot—today."

Roy ate the last few bites of his breakfast standing up and said, "I gotta go to town for a part for the mower. Carl, you finish raking what's cut."

Carl nodded, and out they went.

"Well," Emma said to Henny, who was hunched over his plate, "I can't do it. You'll have to take care of him. He's old and sick, and we can't let him hurt the baby."

A while later, when Emma decided it was time to give Buckley a good-bye pat, both Henny and the dog were gone. "Just as well," she sighed. "No sense getting all riled up. It has to be done."

She assured herself that Henny was a good shot— he'd shot more wildlife than the other two boys put together. He'd have no trouble.

When he came back, she was busy in the pantry and heard him go through the kitchen and dining room to put the gun away on the stair-wall rack. She'd see how things had gone when he came back to the kitchen.

But Henny didn't come back. Instead she heard sobs.

Drying her hands on her apron, Emma hurried to the stairway. She squeezed down beside him on the stairs where he sat, head in hands.

"Oh, Henny." She put her arm around his heaving shoulders.

"Ma, the first shot. . . . It just wounded him. He whined and crawled toward me for help." He sobbed some more, and Emma cried with him. "But I couldn't—I couldn't help him. I had to finish him fast."

Still sobbing, he turned and buried his head, little-boy like, in her shoulder. "I'll never forget that look. He couldn't believe I had hurt him. Oh, Ma! Why'd I hafta do it?"

Emma held him close, "I'm sorry. I'm so sorry."

For that moment, in their mutual grief, their life-circles converged. He had actually turned to her instead of away, as he usually did. Emma longed to keep this fast-becoming-a-stranger son close.

"Oh, Henny, Henny. I wish it hadn't had to be this way. I wish you hadn't had to do it, but you will forget."

He shook his head. "I'll never forget." He sat up and pulled a handkerchief out of his pocket to blow his nose and dry his tears. "Ma, you won't tell Roy and Carl I cried, will you?"

She squeezed his shoulder. "Of course I won't."

Her heart ached as she went about her work, and she longed to let him know, but Henny avoided her eyes at the dinner table. She noticed that he ate very little.

That evening she slipped her arm around his shoulders when he came in to get a drink, but he pulled away and threw the dipper back in the pail. Ignoring the water that splashed out on the floor, he stalked out.

"Oh, Father, what have I done to that boy? Help him! Help him!"

Emma prayed for him again as she walked the floor with the baby that night.

The next morning Henny was more sullen than ever. Most of Emma's thought time was spent on him—until Carl dashed in with the mail.

"Guess what!" he yelled. "Fred is coming home!"

Emma grabbed the letter. "When?"

"First week in August!"

"Think Ed can get home, too?" Roy asked when he came in.

"I hope so, but maybe not. Mail carriers can't take time off from work just like that."

"I don't even remember what Fred looks like," Henny mumbled.

Emma's fork stopped in mid-air. "Why, I suppose you don't. He hasn't been home since Papa died five years ago, and he never really lived at home after you were born. He must seem more like an uncle to you than a brother."

"I remember Fred being kinda quiet," Carl said.

Emma chuckled. "Oh, he can talk plenty. This whole family has the gift of gab. But he never did ta1k loud. Wasn't real strong when he was a boy. Tall, but not muscular like the others.

"Guess that's why he'd end up helping around the house more than the other boys. But he was no sissy!" Emma added quickly. "It was just that he didn't mind doing housework. Why, he could bake better than us women. I remember one time we were over at Ella's, and she had baked sugar cookies. Sugar and shortening were precious those days, and she had tried to make it go as far as possible, so the cookies were mostly flour and awfully thick. Well, Fred picked up one of those fat cookies, looked at it a minute, and said, 'Ella. When I bake cookies, I bake cookies. When I bake biscuits, I bake biscuits.' "

Carl grinned. "Did she get mad at him?"

"Oh, I don't think so. We all had a good laugh, that's all."

When Emma talked to Gertie later, she said, "Oh, won't it be fun to see all those babies together!"

"Want me to start calling everyone and plan a reunion for the Sunday they'll be home?" Gertie asked.

"Oh, would you? I've been thinking about that, but I've got so much to do! I don't know how I'll get this house in shape by then. I never did get the curtains washed this spring—and you know what a good house-keeper Fred's Helen is "

"Oh, Mama, everyone knows what happened this spring—but I'll come and help you a couple days. We've got a whole month, you know."

A few days later, Emma was keeping dinner waiting

for Carl, who had gone to Ziglar's store. "About time," she muttered, when he finally drove in.

The porch door slammed, and Carl yelled, "Ma! Come out here a minute."

What on earth? She bustled out and saw the boys crouching down around something. A puppy!

Carl stepped aside to allow her to get close to it. "Millers said we can have him. They're movin' and can't take him along. He's about three months old and he's real smart, and he'll be a good cow dog 'cause he's a Collie—with a little German Shepherd mixed in. His name's Colonel! How you like him?"

Emma petted his smooth brown head and ruffled his white chest. "Nice white collar." Colonel wiggled and tried to lick her hand, but he didn't jump up on her.

"Look at his tail!" Roy said. "Perpetual motion."

"Colonel is a good name for him," Emma said. "Always thought of a colonel being dignified, and he is. He doesn't jump all over a person like some crazy pups."

A few feet away, Hank held out his hand, palm up. "Come here, boy, come on."

Colonel trotted over, and Hank gathered the fluffy little fellow in his arms.

Haven't seen him grin like that for days, Emma thought. "Carl, go get Jeanie."

Carl held the baby down so the dog could see her, and he sniffed her little feet. She stared and waved her little arms and squealed.

"Well," Emma said, taking Jeanie from Carl, "looks like they might get along. One thing, though. He'll stay outside—all the time." She shook her finger at them. "I don't want him to set one foot in the house! You hear?"

Three heads nodded.

"Well, come on. Let's eat." She led the way in.

The last thing Emma saw in her mind's eye before she fell asleep was Henny—grinning.

Five

The Reunion

"I can't get over how much I've accomplished these last few days," Emma said to Gertie, as she scurried around the kitchen. "Doesn't it feel good to be excited about something?"

Gertie dumped a load of crisply starched curtains on the table. "Guess that's what they call being motivated. There isn't much we can't do, if we want to badly enough."

"Hmmm. I guess that's right." Emma laughed. "Now all I have to do is figure out how to keep wanting to, when we're not having company. I get things done fast when I see them through someone else's eyes."

A moment later she said, "Look at the gladiolas along the driveway. They should be in bloom by the time Fred and Helen come. I'd like to put a nice bouquet up in their room and another one in the front room."

"Or right here on the kitchen table. That's where we are most of the time."

"That's right. Might as well put them where we can enjoy them. I'm going to get those vases and wash them while I'm thinking of it. They've been standing in the cellar since last fall."

It was nice to have Gertie to talk and work with, but one thing they hadn't thought about was Earl's creeping and getting into everything. They tried to pen him in with kitchen chairs laid on their sides, but it didn't take him long to break out. He'd tolerate Jeanie's swing a short while, and then they had to watch him again.

"At least there's no slop pail for him to get into, like when you children were little," Emma said. "I'll never forget how happy I was when Papa told me he was going to put in a sink with a drain when we built this kitchen. But when I saw the men digging that long, deep ditch all the way to the hillside, I felt awfully guilty. All that work, just so I wouldn't have to carry a slop pail!"

Gertie picked up a flat iron from the stove, wet her finger, and quickly touched the bottom. It didn't sizzle, so she tried another one.

"You were never sorry you had it, I bet!"

Emma sprinkled water on a curtain with a snap of her fingers and rolled it tight. "Of course not. You know, Papa even talked about putting in running water, but then he got sick. But after carrying water from the river and the spring all those years, it's luxury enough to have the pump right by the back door."

Gertie changed irons and started another curtain while Emma slid the finished one onto a rod.

"Mmm. Smells nice and fresh. I'm glad you talked me into doing the upstairs ones, too. Another thing we should do is iron a set of sheets for their bed." She held up her hand. "Don't say it! I know. You always iron your sheets. Well, that's fine, as long as you have the energy, but I've been grateful to get pillowcases ironed lately.

"A person has to make choices. I can't do all those things and have enough energy left to be good-natured with the boys and the baby—so I live with wrinkles."

Gertie sighed. "I know—but it's so nice to get into a smooth bed."

Emma arranged the gathers on the curtain and said, "Someday someone's going to invent cloth that doesn't have to be ironed."

"Oh, Ma! Who ever heard of such a thing?"

"Well, I don't know why not. The Bible says, 'Ye have not because you ask not.' Well, I'm going to ask God to help someone invent that kind of cloth. There's lots of things I'd rather do than iron."

The day after Gertie left, Emma hummed and worked and thought. It was good that Fred and Helen were coming now, instead of right after Emmie died.

"I was having such a hard time getting used to mothering that little one," she said to herself. "I wouldn't have been civil company."

It still wasn't easy. The baby woke up several times every night and cried often during the day. The eczema took a lot of care, too, but now Emma's heart was in that care. One night she had dreamed that Emmie had come back—like she had been on a trip somewhere. A flame of joy had swept over Emma, but immediately that joy-flame had been smothered by the thought, "Oh, dear! She'll take Jeanie away!"

The day Fred and Helen were to arrive, Emma was busy trying to do her regular work and still get ready.

Fred had written that they would take the ferry from Muskegon to Milwaukee, stay there over night, and get an early start from Milwaukee in the morning. If they didn't have car trouble they should arrive around six, Roy had said. He should know; he had once driven a new car back from Milwaukee for Ed.

The boys decided to do the milking before supper, but Emma noticed that they each managed to slip in and grab bread and jelly before they went to do chores.

At six Emma turned the chicken again. It was a beautiful golden brown. *If only they'd come before it dries out*, she thought as she looked up the road again.

Any minute now they would be right here—right in front of her eyes. Would Fred look much older? Would little Kermit look a lot like Fred or more like Helen's family? And Everett! Another grandchild she'd never seen. If only they'd come right now!

Emma changed her apron, smoothed her hair, put up a clean roller towel, and washed some spots off the mirror with the soiled one.

Six-thirty. Maybe they had car trouble.

The baby began crying. Emma changed her and put her in her swing and stared out the pantry window again.

She checked the table and poked at the chicken. Pickles! She'd run down to the cellar and get a jar of Fred's favorite dills.

When she came back up, Fred was standing next to the car, stretching his long legs and arms.

Emma caught her breath. "My, he looks like Papa," she said to herself.

A few long strides and Fred's arms were wrapped around her, and then he was holding her at arm's length. "You look good, Ma. I wasn't sure. . . ."

"Oh, I'm fine. So good to see you, boy!"

Emma tried to greet Helen, Kermit, and the baby all at the same time. Kermit allowed his grandma to pat his blonde head and then ran to pet Colonel.

That evening, while Helen put the little boys to bed, Emma sat down with Fred, who was still sipping his coffee.

"I know how hard it must be for you to realize Emmie's going. We were right here through it all, and yet at times I still think it can't possibly be true."

"To me she was still a little girl," Fred said, struggling to control his voice. "She was only fourteen last time I saw her. I could hardly picture her teaching—much less married and a mother."

He cleared his throat. "We knew how she must have suffered. I don't mean only with her illness this spring—I mean getting married and having to quit teaching and all." He shook his head. "That was the last thing I ever expected to have happen to Emmie."

Emma traced the tablecloth pattern with a spoon handle. "Yes, she suffered. She always wanted to do right, and she was so sorry. I suppose there will be some who will always remember that wrong, but those who knew her well knew how contrite she was. She asked for and accepted the Lord's forgiveness."

Emma brushed a few crumbs from the table into her hand and rubbed them into a fine powder in her fingers as she talked. "Oh, I went through a time of thinking if only she hadn't met Ed, and if only she hadn't stayed up at his brother's farm that weekend in July, and if only Ed hadn't been so eager to get married. It was awfully hard not to blame him. Emmie wanted to teach a couple more years before she got married, but Ed was twenty-nine and didn't want to wait."

"That's all past, Ma. What's important now is that little one. Must be hard for you to start all over with a baby again—but she'll be a comfort to you when the boys get married and have their own families. You'll have her to live for."

Emma reached across the table and clasped Fred's hand, but her eyes avoided his. "I get so scared," she whispered. "What if something happens to me?"

They could hear Helen coming down the stairs. Emma met Fred's eyes briefly and withdrew her hand from his reassuring grasp.

"Mother! How thoughtful of you to put the gladiolas in our room. They're beautiful!"

Emma's face flushed. "I was hoping a few more would be in bloom. Maybe tomorrow there'll be more. Now, about tomorrow. Church is at half past nine. I'll take care of the little ones so you can go."

Helen put her hand on Emma's shoulder. "No. We've talked it over. We know you haven't been able to go very often, so I'll take care of the children and Fred will go with you."

It was good to hear Fred's voice singing "Rock of Ages" across the aisle. It had never bothered Emma to sit on the women's side of the church, but today she wished she were sitting with her sons.

During the sermon her mind wandered, pondering all the things she had to do when she got home. Time and again she tried to focus her thoughts on the preacher's words, but then off they would go again.

After the sermon she took out her offering money and dropped it into the *Klinglebointen* as Gust Zielkie extended its long handle down the pew. It had long ago lost the little bell that had hung on the bottom of the velvet bag.

As the organ played, Emma whispered a prayer inside her head. "Oh Father, I'm sorry my mind wandered during the sermon. Forgive me. And today—help me not to miss one single thing that I should do or say. You know I want to be a blessing to my children—like that virtuous woman in Proverbs. Don't let me ever say anything or do anything that would bring shame to them. And, Lord, help me to be loving, even when I get tired. . . ."

She let the words of the last verse of "I Am Trusting Thee, Lord Jesus" flow through her mind:

I am trusting Thee, Lord Jesus;
Never let me fall.
I am trusting Thee forever
And for all.

The tboughts that had plagued her all through the sermon were gone.

Emma sighed. Now, when it was time to go home, her mind was settled on the Lord.

Rev. Fischer gave the benediction, and then suddenly

Emma's friends were all around her, asking about the baby and wishing her well.

Emma and the boys were hardly home when cars began coming.

First Ella and her family arrived and piled out of the car. They bustled across the yard, their arms loaded with bowls of food.

"Ma," Ella called, "the boys want to go swimming down in 'Grandma's swimming hole.' Should I let them go now or make 'em stay and eat first?"

"Oh, let 'em go," Emma said with a wave of her hand. "Who knows when we'll be ready to eat?" She tweaked young Harold's nose as he grinned up at her. "They'll be good and hungry when they get back."

The boys ran off hooting and hollering—Henny right with them.

Emma turned to Ella's husband, Henry, who stood beside her. "That always makes me laugh: 'Grandma's swimming hole'! I never swam in my life; girls weren't allowed to. 'Course Gustie did, anyway. There wasn't much Gustie didn't try."

Al and George trooped in with their wives and children; then John arrived with Ed, Jeanie's dad. John gave Emma a one-armed hug and said, "Here are some lemons for lemonade. I didn't know what to bring."

Gertie's clan arrived next, and then Minnie's. Emma reached out her arms to hold Johnny, her newest grandson.

Minnie's quiet husband, Nels, greeted Emma briefly and hurried into the house. Emma knew he would find an inconspicuous spot and stay there the rest of the day. His severe spine curvature had certainly not kept Minnie from being attracted to him. Emma had hoped their marriage would give him new confidence, but he seemed to be more withdrawn than ever this year.

What a shame, she thought. *That man probably has*

more intelliegence and ability than the rest of us put to-gether. There seemed to be no limit to what he could do, when it came to anything electrical or mechanical.

Emma started to go in again, but waited when she saw Len and Nora drive in. Nora stepped gracefully out of the car. As always, Emma admired her slim ankles and her glowing, dark red hair. If Nora weren't such a loving person, Emma might have been uncomfortable with her dignified city ways.

"Are we the last ones?" Len called across the yard.

"Seem to be," she called back. "Ed and Connie can't come, of course, but everyone else is here."

When Len greeted her he added, "John's been doing real well lately. He hasn't missed work for a long while."

"Oh, I'm glad," she said with a quick glance behind her. "I thought he'd bring Esther today."

Len shrugged. "They've had another lovers' quarrel."

While everyone was sitting around on the lawn, Emma tried to etch all the faces in her memory. All eight sons had Papa's dimple in the chin and large ears but, like a variation of the same music theme, each one was different.

If only Ed could be here—and Emmie. A pang of grief shot through Emma. She could imagine Emmie here, cuddling little Jeanie and talking young-mother talk with the others.

Emma swallowed hard and shook her head. She would not think of Emmie now. Now was the time to take in all that was going on. It might be a long time be-fore they'd all be together again like this.

It didn't bother her not to be involved in conversa-tion. She needed these precious moments to store away the scenes, the sounds. A wave of gratitude swept over her. No conflict among them.

Papa would be so happy. So proud. She could see how

he'd stride around teasing the girls and talking with the boys, glancing her way now and again as if to say, "Aren't they great, Emma?"

She smiled at the children flitting here and there like colorful birds. Young Colonel trotted along, reveling in all the attention—especially from Shirley Emma, who squealed with delight when he tried to lick her.

Len sat down next to Emma with a grin on his face. "Shirley Emma told me, 'He yicks me 'cause he yikes me!'"

Emma laughed. "She is such a little dolly. I love to hear her talk."

Len looked up at the sun. "We'd better get some pictures while the light is good. I'll get Al."

Eventually everyone was rounded up before Al's camera—all except Nels, who stayed under the boxelder tree.

Later, when everyone was back talking in groups here and there, Emma heard loud laughter and went to investigate.

"Come and sit down," Mamie called. "The men are telling hunting stories!"

Emma sat down and winked at Mamie as they watched Carl talk, his hands as busy talking as his mouth.

"John! He's the guy that has the luck!" Carl said. "Remember a couple years ago, when there wasn't any snow? A whole bunch of us—John an' me an' Roy an' Hank—Ed musta been there—and you were there, Len. We'd made drive after drive all day down by that old burning. About four we quit. No snow for tracking— hadn't seen a thing all day. We headed for home feelin' pretty disgusted. John and me an' Len an' Hank took the trail along the edge of the timber. Then John changed his mind and wanted to cut across the swamp to meet the other guys, so we said, 'Go ahead. We ain't goin' that way.' "

John grinned and nodded.

"Well, when we got almost to camp, we heard shooting east of us. So we headed in that direction."

"Yeah," Roy said. "We heard the shots and started toward them, too."

Carl shook his finger at Roy. "We saw you guys coming, and couldn't figure out who'd done the shooting. Then we got up on a little knoll, and there was John down by an old rampike—and what's he doing? Dressin' out a nice buck!"

John grinned. "Eighteen pointer."

"Only deer anyone saw all day," Len said. "That's luck!"

Emma looked at Ed, who was taking it all in. It was good to see him laugh.

"Say Carl," Ed said, "I heard something about a skunk getting you on your confirmation day. What's the story there? Didn't you know better than to tangle with a skunk?"

Those who remembered began to chuckle, and they urged Carl to tell Ed how it happened.

"Skunk hides were bringin' a pretty good price that year. Hank an' I figured if we could catch a couple pair, we could start breedin' them, so we built some pens down by the river. We'd read that if you grab a skunk by the tail and lift its feet off the ground, it can't spray.

"Well, it worked. We caught a couple that way. But that Sunday I ran out quick to check the traps, and I had a nice big feller. I got him out all right and was hiking down toward the pens, but didn't that stinker bite my little finger! I was holdin' him in my right hand and I had a stick in my left, so I just hauled off and hit him one on the nose, so he'd let go my finger."

Carl was laughing so hard he could barely go on. "He let go, all right! Not only my finger, but with his spray apparatus, too! My face was about a foot and a half away, so I got it—good! I couldn't see, I couldn't breathe. I could hear the river about a hundred feet away, and I stumbled and crawled down there and dove in. I washed and washed, and finally I could see enough to get home."

At that point Gertie controlled her laughter long enough to take over. "We had him scrub and scrub and then we doused him with talcum powder and perfume."

Carl wrinkled his nose. "That stuff was worse than the skunk!"

"And we went to church," Gertie continued.

"Shortest confirmation service in history!" Roy added.

"That was one escapade Ma couldn't help finding out about," Gertie said. "But there are probably a few things she doesn't know yet!"

Len laughed. "Like the time Ed got knocked out when we were playing with a raft during the log drive?"

"Yeah," Gertie said, "and the time Ed and John and Roy and I tried to push over that big old tree stump down by the second bend in the river."

"Emmie and I were there, too," Carl said. "We were just little shavers, but I remember."

"I don't think I've heard this one," Emma said.

"That stump must have been about fifteen feet high," Gertie continued, "and every time we went past we'd give it a good shove. Well, this day it was really starting to give way, so we all pushed and got it rocking. But instead of falling from the bottom, a big chunk broke off and came crashing down from above. Hit Ed and knocked him flat. He couldn't move. Couldn't talk. Were we scared!

"John said, 'Bet his back's broke!' and I said, 'Well, if it's broke he'd be bleeding, wouldn't he?' And John said, 'Oh yeah. There'd be a lot of blood.' So we rolled Ed over and pulled up his shirt. He had a couple red spots, but he wasn't even skinned, and we said, 'Well, at least his back ain't broke.' By that time he was gettin his breath back. Since he wasn't bleeding, we figured he was all right, so we yanked him up and told him not to be such a baby."

"And you made Emmie and me promise not to tell," Carl said. "We were hanging on to each other and sha-kin' like leaves in the wind!"

"Poor Ed," Roy said. "No wonder he ended up the smallest of us guys."

Gertie turned to Emma. "Ma? Did you suspect some-thing was wrong?"

"No, I didn't. If Ed was stiff and hurting, I never knew it—and the little ones never said a word." She laughed. "See what you parents have to look forward to!"

All too soon the women began gathering up children and dishes, and Emma was saying goodbye over and over again. It wasn't so hard with those living close—but how would she ever say goodbye to Fred and Helen and the little boys in the morning?

As she prepared for bed that night, she could still hear fragments of the day's happenings—Minnie's chatter, children's laughter, men's voices. She could see moth-ers and their babies, the tenderness in Ed's eyes when he held little Jeanie, Shirley Emma's delight over Colonel, the little girls giggling—she wished there were a way to preserve it all.

Tomorrow Fred and Helen would get into that little black Ford and drive away. Would it be five years again before she saw them? Quick tears came to Emma's eyes, and for a moment she didn't think she could stand to let them go. The little boys—they'd be different people when she saw them again.

She crawled into bed, buried her face in her pillow, and sobbed. Maybe if she allowed herself to cry now it would be easier to hold back the tears tomorrow.

But the next morning, the frying pan blurred through tears as Emma fried potatoes. She ducked into the pantry and dried her eyes on her apron and tried to ignore her aching throat.

As she helped them load the car, she was cheery, but when Fred held her close, sobs blocked all the words she had planned to say. Then they were turning around in the driveway, waving, calling goodbye. . . .

Emma and the boys—Carl, Roy, and Henny—watched until the car disappeared over the hill. Then, without speaking, each went his own direction, to search for a way back to everyday life.

Six

The Old Crab

No matter where Emma turned that morning she saw work—and more work. Given a choice, she would have crept back to bed, but she couldn't ignore the baby's crying or the low diaper pile or the house that certainly looked as though forty people had reveled there the day before.

She'd work hard this forenoon, she decided, but after dinner she'd take a nap. Hadn't her friends at church remarked how tired she looked and cautioned her to take care of herself?

At dinner time she struggled to keep her eyes open.

"Threshers are heading this way," Roy said at the table. "Should be here by Friday."

Emma groaned softly. A threshing crew to feed in a few days. That she didn't need right now. Instead of napping, she'd have to get out and pick the beans, tomatoes, and cucumbers. She'd have Henny pick up windfall apples, even if he did grumble.

Many of the tomatoes were over-ripe. She'd have to can them right away.

Down in the dank cellar, she picked out an armload of jars and started up the stairs. One dropped.

Emma wanted to leave the shattered glass right there on the step, but she made herself go down and sweep it up.

Better get a fire going; she'd need boiling water for washing jars and scalding tomatoes. She reached in the woodbox for kindling—empty. No sense yelling for Henny. He was down in the orchard—or at least he was supposed to be. She'd have to get her own wood.

The baby was screaming when Emma came back in with an armload of wood, but she took time to kindle the fire before she picked her up.

For a while Jeanie was content in her swing, but then she squirmed and fussed. Emma put her on the floor where she squirmed and fussed some more.

By the time Emma hung up the dishpan that night she was so tired she could hardly stagger to bed. If the boys wanted to stay up past dark, they could light the lamp themselves. She was going to turn in, and end this miserable day.

The first thing she heard the next morning was Henny's yell. "Ma! I'm outta socks!" At least he was up!

"Go look in Carl or Roy's drawers," she yelled back.

"Roy's last pair," he said, waving them as he came downstairs. "Carl's out, too."

Emma sighed. She'd planned to wash today anyway, but where were all the socks? One glance at the mending basket solved the mystery. *Should have darned socks while I was visiting last week*, she chided herself.

She didn't even get near the string beans or cucumbers, much less the apples. It took all morning to do the washing and keep the baby quiet.

The phone rang while they were eating dinner, and Roy answered.

When he came back to the table he said, "Could be threshing here Friday." He put the last of the butter on his potatoes. "Frank Knorn'll be at Schellers' tomorrow.

We gotta help there, and the next day at Hank and Ella's."

Carl handed the empty butter dish to Emma. She scowled. "Go get some yourself. Won't hurt you once."

Carl gulped, untangled his long legs from under the table, and headed toward the cellar, looking back over his shoulder.

"Well, what're you starin' at me for? No reason you can't wait on yourselves a little around here," Emma snapped.

After dishes were done, she decided to call Gertie before she started canning tomatoes. She cranked the phone, holding the little black button in so the bell wouldn't ring.

"Number, please," said Central.

"58, please."

The phone rang twice, and Gertie answered. "Oh, Ma! I was going to call you. I feel kinda lonesome today. You rested up after all the company?"

"I guess so. But I just can't get caught up with the work. And the threshing crew'll be here Friday."

"I wish I could help you, but with Earl getting into everything, I'm more bother than I am help."

"I know." Emma sighed. "Just wish the boys would be a little more helpful. They have no idea what it's like for me. . . ."

"We've spoiled them so bad, waiting on them hand and foot."

Emma went back to work feeling sorrier for herself and more lonesome than ever. She worked all afternoon at the tomatoes, except for the time it took to take in the clothes and fold them. Better not sprinkle the starched clothes, she reminded herself. No telling when she'd get time to iron them. She didn't start the beans or cucumbers.

As she set the table for supper, she grumbled to herself. "How am I supposed to dress fryers and bake apple pies and darn socks and finish canning and scrub these dirty floors and still keep the baby happy?"

She could see Ed showing off Jeanie to the others Sunday. "Easy for him to be proud and beaming," she mumbled. "He doesn't have to put up with her day in and day out."

Roy came in with a big rip in his overalls. "Can you sew these before tomorrow morning, Ma?"

"I'm busy. Wear another pair."

He shrugged. "Can't find any without big holes. I thought these would be the quickest to sew."

"Oh, all right! Go change and bring them here." She'd have to let the dishes go and mend the pants first. No fun mending by lamp light.

"They think I'm still a spring-chicken," she grumbled as she pumped her old treadle machine. "Never hear one of them offer me a hand."

As she washed dishes in the twilight, she could hear Henny laughing in the back yard where he was playing ball with Byron Olafson. *All this work to do, and he doesn't see a thing.*

"Henny!" she yelled, dripping dish water across the floor in her haste, "go close the chicken coop. It's almost dark."

"Aw, Ma."

"Aw, Ma, nothing! Do it right now before you forget. It's too dark to play ball, anyhow."

She stomped back into the house and glanced at the clock. *Fine time to be doing supper dishes. Bet every woman for miles around is done—especially everyone my age. They're sitting on their porch swings or in their rockers.*

Evidently getting up on time two mornings in a row was Henny's limit. Wednesday morning Emma had to tap with the broom handle twice. She woke the baby, and still Henny didn't come down.

When he heard her coming up the stairs, he hopped up in a hurry.

She railed at him all the while he laced his shoes.

Henny waited until she stopped to catch her breath and said, "You're an old crab lately. Carl and Roy say so, too." And out he ran.

"Well!" she exclaimed, hands on her hips. "So I'm an old crab, am I? I'd just like to see them put up with what I have to put up with around here!" She couldn't wait to call Ella.

At breakfast Roy said, "Ma, did you close the chicken coop last night?"

"I told Henny to."

Roy scowled at him across the table. "Skunk musta got in. They're still squalking down there, and one's missing."

"Can't depend on that boy at all," Emma muttered as she kneaded bread—the baby crying all the while. She covered the dough, got Jeanie settled in her swing, and went to the phone. She turned the crank. Long, short, short, long.

Ella sounded breathless, as usual. She told Ella what Henny had said. Ella laughed, then quickly apologized. "You're probably still tired from the reunion and the company, Ma. You need help. Why don't you hire one of the Zielkie girls to help cook for the threshers?"

"For goodness' sakes," Emma replied. "I've been cooking for threshers for years. I don't need help. And besides, who's got money for a hired girl these days?"

By noon Emma was aching tired. She got the beans canned while the baby slept, but then the baby woke up crying.

Emma put her in her swing. She cried.

Emma gave her a bottle and laid her down again. She cried.

Emma put her on the floor. She cried.

Finally Emma picked her up and gave her a good shake. "You cry, cry, cry! No matter what I do for you—you cry! You're just a spoiled little stinker, that's what you are!"

The baby stared at her, eyes wide with fear—then her lip trembled, and she began to sob.

Instantly, Emma's frustration and anger vanished. "Oh, *Liebchen, Liebchen!* I'm sorry! It isn't your fault." Emma held the baby close, ignoring the tears running down under her glasses. "I'm just so tired—so discouraged."

With the crying baby in her arms, she sat down in the rocker. "Oh, Father," she wept. "I'm so sorry. Forgive me! I've been thinking about me, me, me, ever since Monday. Some blessing I've been to my family!"

She remembered the fear in baby Jeanie's eyes and cried some more. "I don't want to be like this. Please help me!"

Words floated into her mind, and she whispered them. "I can do all things through Christ which strengtheneth me."

The baby still whimpered.

"It's all right! It's all right!" Emma crooned, and the baby quieted. She tried the swing again. The baby smiled.

The phone ran—two long and two short.

It was Ella, reporting that the threshers wouldn't be around until Saturday.

Emma cleared her throat. "You know, Ella, I've been thinking," she said. "I am going to hire one of the Zielke girls."

Seven

Diphtheria!

Emma didn't even ask Henny to carry wash water for her that October morning. Pumping water would give her an opportunity to take deep breaths of the crisp air and to look so hard at the blue sky she'd remember it on the grayest days of winter.

She'd have to get the pumpkins and squash into the cellar, and dig the carrots and put them in sand, and sort through the apples so the bad ones wouldn't spoil the rest, and wash windows and put on the storm windows. How good it would be to look out at the lawn and way up the hill through nice, clean windows instead of through all those fly specks!

Colonel pranced at her heels while she pumped the next pail of water, and Emma recalled Shirley Emma's delight with him last summer. Word had come through Gertie yesterday that Nora and Shirley were sick, but she didn't know what was wrong. Probably by now they were fine again.

Emma thought about her newest granddaughter, another little Shirley—Ed and Connie's baby—born September 24. She hoped they'd get home next summer.

She dumped another pail and went to check on

Jeanie. Sound asleep. The phone rang, and Emma ran to answer it before it woke the baby.

"Auntie? This is Little Anne."

"Anne, how are you? It's been so long since I've seen you, you'd think we lived a hundred miles apart instead of ten."

They chatted a few minutes, and Emma went back to work smiling. *Nice of Anne to call.* It seemed such a little while ago that Anne was being spoiled by her uncles, just like little Jeanie.

Now I see that it wasn't easy for my mother to raise her, Emma thought. *We just took it for granted—never realized that it must be a struggle for Ma to have a little one in the house again. Now I know how she must have grieved for my sister, Anne, and how sad she felt when Langley put the other two children in an orphanage.*

A chill went through Emma when she remembered. Her mother had been fifty-two when she took Little Anne. And Little Anne had been only thirteen when Ma died.

Emma tried to enjoy the blue sky as she hung out clothes, but she fought worrisome thoughts all forenoon.

After dinner she had Henny drag storm windows out of the tool shed. He washed the outsides of the windows while she did the inside, each pointing out what the other had missed.

What a handsome boy, she thought, shifting her focus to his face. *Maybe the best looking of them all.*

When he caught her staring at him, she made a face at him and pointed out another spot he'd missed.

While Henny went to get more windows, Emma took a moment to enjoy their accomplishment. She gazed out of the pantry window, wondering what colors she would use to paint that scene the window framed.

The sky, she noticed, was many shades of blue. The

woods peering up over the top of the hill were dark, dark green; the road, red-brown. The pasture—why it looked as though someone had thrown down an old gray comforter with holes in it where some wool was poking out. One of these years, as the sod crept over them, those boulders might be completely covered.

What would she do about the shine of the creek? Paint it white? The garden was scrappy now in fall, but she wouldn't paint it that way. She'd make it a spring garden, with rows of different shades of green. But that wouldn't be right with the other fall colors. Have to make it all spring or all fall.

Emma shook her head. *Me, an artist! Silly thought!*

A car drove in the driveway just then, interrupting her daydreaming. John! What on earth? He never came in the middle of the week. Had Len fired him?

John kept his head down as he walked toward her. He put his arm around her shoulder and said, "Where are the boys?"

"I don't know where Roy and Carl are. Henny's here. Why?" She turned to call to him. "Henny! Go find the boys."

John waited until Henny had run towards the barn. "Ma." His voice broke. "Little Shirley Emma's dead. Diphtheria. Nora's got it, too."

"No!" Emma cried, collapsing in John's arms. "Not that little dolly!"

When the boys came, they found their mother and brother sitting at the table staring at coffee cups. John told them the news, and they sat down in stunned silence.

Emma hugged each one in turn. "I'd better call Gert," she said.

John shook his head. "I stopped on the way down."

"I'll call Ella then."

The sun was low before all the family had been reached.

The boys went to do chores, and Emma remembered the diapers on the line. Could it have been only a few hours ago she was singing, carefree, as she pumped water?

Nora with the silver-bell laugh. Nora with the fair skin and glowing red hair.

"Oh, Father, pull her through," Emma prayed as she went to get Jeanie's diapers. "Len, the other girls, her mother—they all need her." She dabbed her eyes with a diaper. "God, I don't know why these things happen, but I know you don't want them to. I feel like you're crying right with us. You are a God of love. I don't understand why some must die and others are spared, but please, make Nora well, and don't let the others get sick!"

John called from Phillips the next morning to say that Nora was still in critical condition. They could come and view Shirley Emma's little body through a window before the funeral service.

Surely, Emma thought, this was one of the saddest days of their lives. A glimpse through the window and a brief grave-side service, and they were on their way home again. She had longed to comfort Len, but fear of contagion kept people at a distance. Nora's condition, they were told, had not improved.

"Father," Emma sighed, "I'm prayed out and I'm cried out. I rest in Your Almighty arms."

The report was the same for the next three days.

They worked automatically and spoke little—at least the boys did. Emma spent a great deal of the time either answering the phone or reporting Nora's condition to others.

"I feel like the whole world is holding its breath," she told Al and Mamie the third day. "Even little Jeanie senses something's wrong. The boys don't play peek-a-boo with her or toss her around, and she has seen me cry so much. She has the saddest look on her little face."

The fourth evening, as they sat around the table talking, Emma said, "Surely Nora must feel all these prayers. Len, too."

Henny rolled up the *Youth's Companion* he was reading and banged the table with it. "Well, they ain't feelin' mine! I ain't prayin' to a God who kills little kids!"

Emma was so startled she couldn't get a word out.

"Why'd He let her die?" Henny demanded. "He can do anything, can't He?"

Roy looked questioningly at Emma.

Henny shoved his chair back, got up, and paced the floor, smacking the magazine into his palm. "Ain't that right? God can do anything?"

Emma laid down her knitting. "Yes. He can."

Henny's eyes blazed. "Well then, why didn't he make her well?"

Emma cleared her throat. "You answer me something first. Does God make us do anything? Does He like everything we do?"

Henny stopped pacing. "No—no. But what's that got to do with it?"

"It means that He can do anything, but He doesn't always. He could have created us so we had to obey Him, but He didn't. We can make up our own minds what we want to do or believe, isn't that right?"

Henny nodded.

Roy and Carl were hanging on every word.

"Don't you see, boys?" Emma said, jabbing the air with a knitting needle to emphasize her words. "If God controlled us, we would automatically love Him, and what kind of love would that be? Love isn't love unless we can choose to love."

Roy and Carl nodded, but Henny sat down and scowled.

"Don't see what that's got to do with Shirley Emma dyin'."

Emma sighed a long sigh and leaned her head back against the rocker. "I know it isn't simple. I don't know why God does what He does, but I know this—He is a loving God! He grieves when we don't live the way that is best for us—the way He tells is us best in His word. Things started going wrong way back in Eden, because man wanted his own way, and it's still goin' on. We can't blame God for what is caused by sin."

Henny scraped his chair back and flung the magazine on the table. "It don't make sense to me," he muttered and stomped off to bed.

Carl and Roy exchanged glances, said goodnight to Emma, and followed Henny up to bed.

"Oh, Father," Emma prayed, alone in her rocking chair, "grief over death is hard, but grief over a hard heart is worse. Help that boy!"

The fifth day dragged by. The boys ate supper, talking only when necessary, and went to do chores.

Emma sat at the table sipping lukewarm coffee. The baby sat on her lap, banging a spoon on the table. The phone rang, and she put Jeanie down and hurried to answer it.

"Nora's better!" Gertie cried. "The doctor says she's going to live!"

Emma ran down to the barn, crying, "Thank you, Lord! Thank you, Lord!" all the way.

"Boys!" she yelled. "Nora's better! She's going to live!"

She didn't stop to see how they responded. There were too many calls to make.

Eight

Baby's First Christmas

Henny pushed the Montgomery Ward catalog across the table, keeping his finger on the item he wanted Emma to see. "Look at this, Ma. It's called a 'come-back.' Think Jeanie would like it?"

"Hmmm. 'Come-back returns when rolled,'" Emma read. She held the catalog at a different angle to catch the lamp's feeble rays. "Three inches in diameter, it says. She'd be able to hold it. I think she'd like that."

"Should I order it for her?"

"Where you going to get forty-nine cents? That's half a day's wages!"

Henny chewed his lip. "Figured I'd trap weasels. Bet I'll get a whole bunch of 'em before Christmas. One thing, though—gotta stretch 'em and ship 'em. Might not get paid in time."

Emma smiled. "When I see the weasels, you get a loan."

Henny grinned. "Gotta buy your present in town, so you won't see it on the order blank."

Emma smiled to herself. Seldom did she see her sullen boy excited and thinking about someone else.

But the thought of Christmas was painful. She

ached for Len and Nora and remembered the first
Christmas Papa was gone. They'd all tried to be cheery,
and to remember the real reason for joy—but they
missed him so much.

All the Christmases since had been a struggle. The
boys feigned delight over her handmade gifts of socks
and mittens and the whistles and trifles they gave each
other, but even putting up a tree had become a chore. It
would be much worse this year, with Emmie gone—
unless the baby made a difference.

A few days later Carl tramped in and said, "Wait'll
you see the swell tree I found. Balsam, like you always
want, and it's perfect. Think we can order some new
candy cherries and beads and stuff?"

He gave Jeanie's swing a push. "Wait'll you see that
Christmas tree, kid!"

Emma smiled as she watched Jeanie giggle at Carl's
silly faces. Yes, the baby would make a difference—but
Emma still dreaded the empty space no one but Emmie
could fill. As she put *Pfeffernuesse* in baking pans, she
could suddenly see the boys and Emmie bantering as
they trimmed the tree last year. Grief, like an unexpected
ocean wave, caught her off balance. She ran to the pantry so the baby wouldn't hear her, and let the tears come.
How would she get through Christmas without Emmie's bubbling laugh?

The afternoon of Christmas Eve, Carl put the tree in
the old stand Papa had made of crossed two-by-fours. He
set it on the porch, ready to bring into the house after
the church program.

"Baby going bye-bye," Emma told Jeanie. She sang as
she dressed her:

Hang up the baby's stocking
Be sure and don't forget
For the dear little dimpled darling

Has never seen Christmas yet.

Roy came in smiling and joined her in the next verse:

I told her all about it.
She opened her big, blue eyes.
I'm sure she understood it
'Cause she looked so cunning and wise.

That night, as the huge tree was lighted with a candle attached to a long pole, Jeanie's little eyes grew round. No crying tonight, but she did wiggle as the children spoke their pieces.

After the service, folks large and small clustered around to pat her shiny hair and remark how she was growing. The baby gave a little smile and a big yawn, and Emma laughed.

"Hope she's still that sleepy when we get home."

"Go ahead and get the tree in," Emma told the boys as she undressed Jeanie. "She doesn't know what's going on." But they refused to bring it in until she was safely in bed. It must be a complete surprise.

When Emma came out of the bedroom, the tree was in its place, and the boys were turning it this way and that to find the best side.

"It's a lovely tree," Emma assured Carl, as Henny and Roy teasingly pointed out flaws.

Emma went to get the ornament box, and Carl yelled, "Ma! Hank's eating the popcorn we strung last night."

"Oh, you boys! Hush now, or you'll wake the baby."

Roy put "O Come All Ye Faithful" on the phonograph, and Emma hummed along as she polished fragrant delicious apples for her cut glass bowl.

Last year Emmie had explained to Ed, "We've had apples in that bowl every Christmas, as long as I can remember." And he had squeezed her hand and said, "I like that. Next year, when we have our own home, we can start our own traditions."

But they didn't even have one Christmas in their own home, Emma thought bitterly.

"Hey, Ma?" Carl called, interrupting her thoughts. "Is this candle far enough away from that branch?"

"I don't think so." She got up and helped him find a better place for the candle holder, then went to get the box she had hidden in the cream-separator room. She opened the little brown bags of hard candy, chocolate drops, peanut brittle, and mixed nuts and put some out, telling the boys just to take a sample, so there'd be plenty for tomorrow.

The boys brought out their gifts for Jeanie—unwrapped so she could see them right away—and tissue paper wrapped packages for each other.

Henny placed the red and blue come-back well in front of the large roly-poly Carl had bought, and frowned at the fluffy brown teddy bear from Roy. "Wonder if she'll even see it," he muttered.

Emma brought out the rag doll she had sewn during Jeanie's nap times, thinking of the many rag dolls she had made through the years.

"Now, don't bring her out in the morning until we get the candles lit," Carl reminded Emma.

Then, of course, they had to light the candles. Even Roy and Henny had to admit it was one of the prettiest trees they had ever had. After a few minutes' admiration they blew out the candles and trooped upstairs, reasoning like little children that the sooner they got to bed, the sooner morning would come.

Emma refilled the candy and nut bowls—she hadn't really expected the boys to stop with a sample. One more stick of wood in each stove, and her day's work was done. She sat down a moment and took deep breaths of the balsam and candle fragrance. But tonight they evoked grief, not the happy memories they once had inspired. She felt it growing, gathering deep within her, and she fled to the bedroom.

"Father, help me! Don't let me spoil the day for the boys—and for Ed, when he comes. And Father, comfort Len and Nora. Help them through tomorrow. . . ."

Before she blew out the lamp, she tucked the covers higher around Jeanie's little shoulders and kissed her rough little forehead. "God bless this baby," she murmured. "Such a little honey."

No problem getting Henny up this morning, Emma thought as she tied her old pink flannel robe. She could hear the boys tiptoing around and smell the sulphur from matches as they lit the candles. One of them was shaking down the ashes in the heater stove and putting in wood, and another was doing the same in the kitchen.

She peeked around the doorway. "Merry Christmas, boys! You ready?"

Carl scurried in from the kitchen as Emma lifted Jeanie out of her crib and wrapped a blanket around her. "It's Christmas Day, honey! Let's go see."

Jeanie snuggled against Emma's shoulder, but when Emma turned her toward the tree, up came the little head. Her eyes flew open.

Emma tore her eyes away from the baby's face to watch the grinning boys. She put Jeanie down on the floor, blanket and all.

Henny was beside her in an instant, demonstrating the come-back. Jeanie waved her little arms and made happy sounds and tried to grab it when it rolled back to her. Then the roly-poly caught her eye and Carl quickly showed her how to set it wobbling.

Roy stood smiling, arms folded, watching them. He caught Emma's eye and winked. Jeanie would find the teddy bear and rag doll eventually.

When it was time for the others to open gifts, Jeanie was not about to sit quietly. She crept around scattering paper and boxes, and then grabbed a low branch of the tree.

"No!" Emma scolded. "See! Hurts fingers!" She deliberately stuck Jeanie's little fingers into the prickly needles.

A moment later Jeanie grabbed for a low-hanging ornament.

"No!" said Emma, slapping the little hand.

Jeanie's merry little face contorted, and she sobbed.

"Don't look at me like that," Emma told the boys. "She has to learn."

"We coulda put it up on a table this year," Carl said.

"Nonsense! Never put the tree out of reach for any of you."

Ed came well before noon and enlisted the boys' help unloading the car.

"What's Daddy's little girl got? Show Daddy!" Ed said, looking down at Jeanie, who was busily playing with her toys. "Pick her up for me, will you, Roy?"

At times Emma forgot that Ed wore a heavy brace. His back had been broken while he was in the army, and a portion of leg bone had been grafted into his spine. *Oh, dear*, she thought. *It must be troubling him again*.

"Wait till you see what Daddy brought you!" he said. "Carl, want to open that big box?"

"A rocking pony!" Carl exclaimed.

It was made for a tiny child—with a frame around the seat to hold the little rider in. Emma ran her hand around the bent-wood circle that enclosed the seat and examined the handles protruding from the horse's head.

Jeanie was so tiny she couldn't reach the foot board or the handles.

"We'll fix that," Emma said, tucking a blanket behind her. "Won't be long and she'll be rocking herself."

Ed pointed to two large, flat boxes. "Those are yours, Mother."

Emma sat down and opened one. It was a large portrait in an oval frame. "Oh, Ed! Thank you! My, weren't you handsome in uniform!"

Henny whistled. "That frame real gold?"

Ed smiled. "Gold plated, I guess." He rubbed his hands together nervously as he waited for Emma to open the second box.

She reached for it, her heart thumping. "Help me Father," she prayed silently as she lifted the top off the box.

"Oh, Emmie!" she said. Her voice broke at the sight of the nearly life-size image.

Ed haltingly explained that it had been taken from her class picture. "I wanted one of her smiling—she was rarely so sober. But we couldn't find any other picture clear enough to enlarge."

"It's beautiful, Ed. You know I'll treasure them both."

The boys took a quick look and disappeared.

They didn't need such a vivid reminder, Emma thought. *I've got to think of some way to lift everyone's spirits.*

But before she could think of anything, Colonel barked. Someone was coming.

"It's Al and Mamie and the kids," Henny yelled.

"Thank you, Lord," Emma whispered, as she went to welcome them.

They had hardly gotten inside the house, when in walked George with a grin on his face.

"Guess what we got for Christmas?" he asked Al's children.

"A b-i-g sled?" little Art said, stretching his arms as wide as they would go.

"Nope!" George said, tossing Art in the air. "We got a brand new baby girl. Her name is Ardis."

Little Art didn't look a bit impressed, but Emma and Mamie plied George with questions.

That evening, Emma leaned back and closed her eyes, enjoying the quiet. Only an occasional snap of the fire and the clock ticking. The boys had gone to bed, but she needed to relive the day—Christmas, 1924.

She smiled as she remembered the baby's astonishment, the candles reflected in her eyes, and Henny and Carl down on the floor with her.

And that precious moment of wordless communication with Roy over the younger ones' heads. What would she do without that blessed boy? *Really should stop thinking of him as a boy*, she thought. *He's twenty-three tomorrow. One of these days he'll want a home of his own—a wife. But surely not for a long time.*

She thought of Ed, so delighted with Jeanie in her rocking horse. He didn't seem strong, physically or emotionally, and Emma's heart ached for him.

And what a shock to see Emmie's face. Someday, Emma knew, it would be comforting to look at that nice, clear likeness . . . someday. Thank goodness, Al's family and George had come when they had.

"Father, thank you," she whispered. "Only that one rough spot. But I'm sorry we didn't celebrate your birthday, Jesus, the way I'd have liked to. We thought only about ourselves, not you.

"Next year, help us make Christmas a day that will please you. I want to teach little Jeanie all about you. I want her to love you. Please let me be with her until she doesn't need me anymore. And Father, help me be a blessing to my whole family. . . ."

Nine

Another Year

Emma buttoned the last button on Jeanie's little brown and black shoes; then she stuck the button hook in the washstand drawer and lifted the little girl so she could see herself in the mirror.

"Look at that big girl! She's a whole year old today!" Emma kissed her little cheek. "Now we'll go put on the new dress your daddy sent you, and you'll look pretty when Auntie Gertie and the boys come."

The first thing Gertie said after arriving was, "Look at her face! She's all smooth!"

Emma beamed. "Not a sign of a scar, either. She still has some spots behind her knees and in her elbows, but that's not so bad."

"I brought my camera," Gertie said. "Let's take the kids' pictures while they're still clean and the sun is high."

Emma carried Jeanie out and stood her up in a sunny spot, but she immediately plopped down on the grass. Her cousins Clyde and Earl raced around, and she tried to creep after them.

"Gert! Just take it with her sitting down, or she'll be a mess!" The two women watched the little ones playing on the damp grass.

"I can't remember the lawn ever greening out like this by the end of March," Gertie commented. "Doesn't seem possible that last year at this time we were having a blizzard."

Emma sighed. "When Ed called that morning to say the baby had come, I could just see us going up there to visit them. I imagined how proud Emmie would be. . . ."

Gertie put her arm around Emma's shoulder, and they walked toward the house. "It's been a hard year, Ma. This one will be easier."

Al's and Ella's families came for the celebration, too. As Emma rushed around serving the birthday cake, she caught snatches of conversation about "creation" and "evolution" and the governor of Tennessee, but she couldn't piece it all together. When everyone was served, she finally sat down beside Al and asked him it was all about.

"Seems there are teachers teaching that man came from apes instead of being created by God. The governor of Tennessee just signed a bill making it unlawful for a teacher in that state to teach anything except the Bible's teaching of creation."

"Well, I should hope so! I hope every state passes a law like that."

Al shook his head. "Looks like we can expect a lot more of this evolution teaching. Lots of people would rather believe Darwin's theories than the Bible."

"Well, land's sakes! All they have to do is look around them, and they can see all this didn't happen by chance. I can't imagine anyone believin' that."

"Nels says he does," Gertie said, keeping her eyes on her plate.

Emma shook her head. "Poor Nels. Sometimes smart men can be so foolish. But he's young yet. . . . He'll change his mind."

For several days the conversation haunted Emma. What kind of a world would these little ones be living in, if such ideas grew? But each time, before she worried herself into a dither, she cut off the fearful thoughts with a whispered prayer: "Father, take care of these little ones. I trust you!"

Emma worked in the yard that May remembering what Gertie had said—this year would be easier. She agreed—until she had chased Jeanie down the driveway several times.

As she worked, she kept up a running monolog. "That's bark from the tree. Ichh! Don't put it in your mouth. Oh, look here! An angle worm. Put out your hand. Look at him wiggle! You don't like him? Aw, he's a nice little worm."

She had forgotten what it was like to see the world through a little one's eyes. She picked a dandelion and turned to hand it to Jeanie, but the child was gone.

"That little rascal! How could she disappear so fast?"

Emma looked in the driveway, on the west side of the house, and behind the lilac bush, calling as she walked. Then she heard a high little voice calling from the front of the house, "Ma! Ma!"—just as the boys would call her.

She found Jeanie by the big, old honeysuckle bush, her left foot stuck between its low branches. Emma couldn't help laughing as she pulled Jeanie out and gave her a hug. She'd have to tell the boys about it at suppertime.

One day about the middle of June, Mamie called and invited Emma to come celebrate Al's birthday.

"How would it be if Al comes and gets you about one? You could spend the afternoon with us, and the boys could come over for supper. We so seldom get a chance to visit."

Emma felt guilty that day, as she shut the kitchen door on all her work. But spending time with other members of her family was important, too, she reminded herself.

Emma could almost smell the coffee perking as she thought of Al's cozy green house. It was always pleasant to visit with Mamie, with her soft Norwegian accent. She was rarely without a smile and didn't have to look hard to find a reason to giggle like a schoolgirl. It made Emma feel good just to think about being there.

Al sat down with the women to have a cup of coffee. "If anyone wants me, they'll come to the house," he said. "I never thought the time would come when blacksmithing would be a dying trade, but I see it coming."

Emma's brow furrowed. "What will you do? Get more cows?"

Al shook his head. "No. Think I might try the city. Muskegon, maybe. There's no sense sittin' and scowlin' at the cars going by—might as well make em."

Mamie poured coffee without comment. Emma knew she'd hate to leave her elderly parents, who lived just a few miles away.

"Oh, I've got news," Emma said brightly. "John and Esther are getting married next month. Roy's going to be best man."

A1 grunted. "Hope they get along better after they're married than they do now."

"Now, Al," Mamie chided. "Those were just lovers' quarrels."

Emma sighed. "I hope so. Esther simply isn't a happy person."

Mamie leaned closer to Emma. "Are we invited to the wedding?"

Emma shook her head. "I'm not even invited. They're getting married in the parsonage."

"Oh. . . . I didn't know." Mamie put her hand on Emma's.

"I don't know much about Esther's family, except that her father is dead and she has one brother."

The screen door slammed, and the boys dashed. "Gramma!" Art yelled. "Wanna pick strawberries? There's lots of 'em."

Emma hugged Art with one arm; and Paul with the other. "I'd love to, if you'll help watch Jeanie."

Mamie gave each one a tin cup and followed them out. "We can't have Al's birthday cake without wild strawberries now, can we?"

"I should say there's lot of 'em!" Emma exclaimed when they reached the edge of the woods across the driveway. She picked a stem laden with four brilliant red berries and twirled it in her fingers. "There's enough for a million shortcakes."

Paul gave Jeanie a berry. She put it in her mouth, squeezed her eyes shut, and shivered. Art tried to give her another one, but she ran off. The children played and chased each other, stopping now and then to drop a few berries in their cups.

Emma straightened her back and watched Al hike toward the blacksmith shop. "I should have realized that with everyone buying cars, there isn't as much horse-shoeing. But there'll always be work horses."

Mamie shook her head. "Al says it won't be many years till farmers will be using tractors in the fields instead of horses."

Emma laughed. "Oh, that boy! Who ever heard of such a thing?"

"Well, August Johnson has had a tractor for several years, and so has Edgar Weiland."

"Yes, but I thought they just used them to haul things. I never thought they could use tractors in the fields like horses. I'm way behind. I guess sometimes I don't pay attention because I don't like to see things change. I don't even want to think about you moving."

Mamie straightened up and said, "Look at little Jeanie playing right with the children. She isn't a baby anymore!"

Emma nodded and said pensively, "Yes . . . but there are so many years to go until she's on her own."

Mamie's smile faded. "I think I know how you feel. I was so scared when I was sick, and Ruby was just a baby—Art! Be careful!" she yelled.

Too late. He and Paul were pulling the wagon with their little sister and Jeanie in it, and had turned it short. Out tumbled the little girls!

Emma reluctantly gathered up the deep feelings she had been about to share and thrust them back down beyond reach. Someday there would be another opportunity to talk about them.

It seemed like summer had hardly begun when it was threshing time again.

"I've come a long way since last year," Emma said to herself as she watered house plants in the bay window. Instead of feeling overwhelmed, she was excited. "I'll cook a real good dinner," she decided. "I don't want my boys to be ashamed."

She smiled as she thought of the old engine coming up over the hill with its PUTT, putt, putt, putt, putt . . . PUTT. How that top-heavy old rig would rattle and squeak its way down to the threshfloor. Old Frank would back the tractor up the hillside and anchor it in the same old holes and stretch that big belt from tractor to threshing rig. Load after load of oat bundles would be fed onto its conveyer and disappear into its noisy innards, while sack after sack of oats would be drawn from its side and straw showered up into the loft through the blower pipe.

She'd take Jeanie down to watch it—if it didn't scare her.

Emma moved the fern to a sunny spot and turned a geranium that was leaning toward the light. *May as well call Gertie while I'm by the phone,* she thought.

Gertie offered to come and help while the threshers

were there, or at least keep Jeanie from getting under foot.

"I was just remembering those awful days I put myself through last year at threshing time," Emma said with a sigh. "All I have to do is start feeling sorry for myself, and I'm a goner."

"Oh, Ma. Everyone has a right to feel sorry for herself now and then," Gertie said with a laugh. "I figure I might as well. No one else does."

"But we can't be loving when we're all tied up with self-pity!" Emma protested.

"Who says we've got to always be loving?"

"Why, Gert! You know what the Bible says about love—"

"Ma, I gotta go. Earl's screaming."

Emma hung up the phone and shook her head.

"Father," Emma whispered. "I fear for her. She's got to have things perfect, and she works till she almost drops and then gets down because no one feels sorry for her. Please help her see that old Satan just waits till we get tired to get us thinking wrong. Help me remember that, too!"

Emma had hardly caught up with her regular work after threshing when the corn froze, and she was faced with cooking for the silo-fillers.

Again Gertie said she'd come and stay a couple days, if the boys didn't mind having Clyde around.

"Oh, I don't think they mind," Emma assured her. "They said he was no bother at threshing time. He'd sit wherever they told him to and stay there."

Gertie chuckled. "He was born an old man. Wait till Earl gets that age—I'm afraid he won't be as welcome."

Gertie took the little ones out on the lawn while she husked a whole wash-boiler full of corn and peeled a huge kettle of potatoes. Earl and Jeanie rolled and tumbled like a pair of cubs.

Emma watched from the window and smiled. It was good for Jeanie to have other children to play with.

While dinner cooked, they took the little ones down by the silo to watch the wagons pull in and the corn ride the conveyer into the cutter and blower. Jeanie clung to Emma's neck and stared at the pipe running up the outside of the silo where chunks of corn cobs rattled and thunked and took their final plunge into the silo along with the juicy stocks.

Like a stone gathering momentum as it rolls down hill, the weeks went by faster and faster until suddenly it was time to prepare for Christmas once again.

The holiday came and went in a blur of activity, and once more it was New Year's Eve.

As Emma sat thinking over the past year, she realized that this had been the first Christmas since Papa got sick that she had really felt happy—thanks to that little busybody Jeanie.

She shivered as a gust of wind set the window panes trembling. She laid her knitting aside and put wood in both stoves. The fragrance of the tree candles still hung in the air, and the tinsel glittered as it caught the glow of the fire.

Emma tiptoed into the bedroom and tucked the covers close around Jeanie's neck. "Bless her little heart," she whispered. A few more months, and she'd be two.

Only two. At least sixteen more years to go.

Emma sat down wearily and began to take out her hair pins. *How wise God is*, she thought, *to keep the future from us. How could we ever keep going if we knew all that would happen?*

But tonight she wouldn't think about what might happen. Tonight she'd think about the happy days just past.

She closed her eyes and watched the scenes in her mind's eye—long-legged Carl sprawled out on the floor, building block towers for Jeanie. Henny, chair tilted back on two legs, arms folded across his chest, laughing at Jeanie's antics.

And her favorite scene: Roy holding Jeanie in the rocker facing the lighted Christmas tree, singing carols. Each time a song ended, her little hand would come up and pat his cheek, and she'd say, "More! More!" *What a good daddy he'll make someday*, she thought as she watched.

The only painful part of the holidays had been Ed's visit. He tried to be cheerful and to win Jeanie's affection, but he was a stranger to her. When anyone put her in Ed's arms, she'd wiggle right down again, and he'd fight back tears. Poor man.

"I get so mad at myself," Emma had told Gertie. "Ed has never said a critical word, but I'm so self-conscious and tense when he comes. I'm always afraid I'm not doing things right."

The clock struck nine. Time to get to praying.

Day after day, Emma prayed for her family as a group and for whoever had special needs. But tonight she planned to pray for each one of them individually, and that would take awhile.

Her lips moved as she held each one—from Al down to Henny—up to the Lord. Then she prayed for her brothers and sisters, for President Coolidge, for Rev. Fischer, for Dr. McKinnon, the mailman, the cream hauler, and the neighbors all around the mile square block and beyond.

She yawned, combed her hair, and braided it in one long braid. Dreamily, she took a few long hairs from the comb and wound them around the end of the braid to secure it.

"Then there's me, Lord," she continued. "I'm not proud of the way I lived this past year—of all the times I worried and was afraid . . . and the times I snapped at the boys and was impatient with little Jeanie. And most of the time I forgot about the patterns you gave me from Proverbs and First Corinthians."

"I know some things that virtuous woman did, I can't do." She smiled at the thought of going out and buying a field. Imagine the boys' faces if she came home and told them, "I've just bought a forty back of Hank and Ella's."

Abruptly, Emma brought her thoughts back in line, but she didn't feel ashamed. The Lord probably enjoyed her little flight of fancy.

"Lord, I don't know my own heart. Do I want to be like this woman so my children will praise me? I don't mean to look for praise, but I do want to be a blessing to them.

"And more than that, I want to be a blessing to you. I can't do anything to please you in my own power, but You live in me." Tears brimmed over as she said, "Oh, Lord, I want to be what you want me to be. I want Your will to be my will. I want to love with Your love."

The clock struck ten.

"Father, Jesus, Holy Spirit—I love You. I thank You for loving me. Whatever happens in 1926, I know You'll be with me."

Emma sat quietly, bathed in God's love and peace, until a blast of wind shook the windows. Automatically, she put wood in the stoves, undressed, and snuggled into bed, His peace still enfolding her.

Ten

Quickly Go the Years

Only three plates on the big old table. The holidays were over, and Roy had gone back to the lumber camp and Carl back to Phillips, where he worked for Len most of the winter.

Emma sighed as she finished setting the table. Work, they needed. The few remaining cows brought barely enough money to buy flour, sugar, oatmeal, kerosene, and gas for the car. "Why did I ever let Gertie and John talk me into selling so many of the cows after Papa died?" she asked herself again, as she had so often.

Meanwhile, Emma was glad when Carl could find work and be independent, though she missed his easy-going humor. And she whole-heartedly agreed that Roy should work in camp. How else would there be money for machinery repairs or a new car? The model T Ford that Roy and Emmie had bought wouldn't run forever.

But it wasn't easy to take care of the stock with just Henny's help. His heart was in his trap line. One moment Emma was concerned about him, out in the bitter cold all day with only frozen sandwiches to eat, but the next moment she wanted to shake him for not putting the farm work first.

She scowled out the window. If only he'd get home at a decent hour.

The evening blue of snow and sky gave way to gray and black, and only by cupping her hands around her eyes as she pressed her face to the window could she see out at all.

Still no Henny.

Maybe he had an accident. No! I won't think like that!

She stirred the stew and moved it back on the stove. If only Papa were here! She wouldn't have to be concerned about the cattle and chickens and the size of the wood pile, or put up with Henny's grouchiness. Papa would never stand for that.

She gave her head a sharp shake. *Plain foolish to think like that! Got to think about what to do right now—the way things are!*

She'd start doing the chores, even if he did get mad. She had done that one day last week when he had been late.

Henny had slammed into the barn yelling, "You know I'm comin'. Why the heck can't you wait?" He had waved his arms toward the cattle. "They ain't starvin' to death!"

But Emma couldn't stand to think of those animals going hungry or of poor Molly, recently freshened, waiting to be milked. She chuckled. Couldn't expect a man to understand the pain that a delay in milking caused.

"Come on, *Liebchen!*" she said as cheerily as she could. "Let's go see the kitties and the sheep and the bossy cows!"

She stuck Jeanie's little non-cooperative arms in sleeves and stuffed her hands into mittens. Then she dragged the little girl up onto her lap and pulled overshoes on twisting, turning feet. As she tried to buckle the stiff metal buckles, pain shot through her arthritic fingers.

Oh! To be able to dress herself and walk out of the house, alone . . . unhampered.

Jeanie's smiling little face beamed up at her, and Emma's eyes misted. She slammed her mind's door and hugged Jeanie close.

Then she lit the lantern, took Jeanie's hand, and picked her way over the icy bumps, accompanied by their tall shadows.

Inside the barn Emma sang, "Where He leads me I will follow, my dear Saviour I will follow. . . ." She laughed as the old, gray mama cat escaped Jeanie's grasp.

Quickly she milked Molly. She patted her flank. "There, now! That feels better, doesn't it?"

Emma was glad she had started the chores. The warm barn and familiar odors eased the tension of waiting. She could handle most of the work herself, except for throwing down hay and a few other things. The trouble came later, when her dwindling energy supply ran out long before her housework was done.

She was dragging hay to the cows when Henny came in, whistling. She shook her head. Never did know what kind of mood he'd be in.

"Must have had some good catches today."

"Yup!" he answered.

She wished he'd tell her about the animals, the way she heard him tell Floyd Olafson when he came over. Where had he learned so much about nature? Certainly not from books.

Oh, well, she thought, *at least he's in good humor tonight.*

It didn't hurt Emma's feelings at all when the spring thaw came early, breaking up the skidding roads and ending the woods-work. Roy was home again.

He brought her Mayflowers he had found in the woods for her birthday, April 18. Emma put them in the cut glass toothpick holder and promised herself she'd take Jeanie up to the stone piles when the spring flowers were in bloom.

On a sunny afternoon two weeks later, she took Jeanie's hand and started across the stubble field east of the house. "Let's go pick pretty flowers."

But Jeanie didn't care if she went any farther than the drainage ditch that ran through the field.

"No! No! The water's too cold. Come on! Let's find flowers." Emma had to grab her before she stepped in the water and carry her the rest of the way.

Emma set her down in the midst of the first clump of pale pink Mayflowers. "Look, *Liebchen*. Pretty flowers!"

But Jeanie was off yelling, "More fowers, more fowers," each time she found another patch.

Emma smiled and let her run. Some year she'd marvel at their downy stems and delicate colors—a miracle after the lifeless cold.

"Ma! Ma! Snow!" Jeanie yelled.

Snow? *Can't be any snow left*, Emma thought as she strolled over to see.

"Oh, honey! That's not snow! That's a rock with mica in it. It sure does sparkle like snow." Where had the glacier found that rock—and all the others now partly embedded in the sod.

They walked back, Emma carrying Jeanie until they crossed the ditch again. She took deep breaths of the cool, fresh air.

"I'm happy!" she said to herself. "I'm really happy."

Spring hurried by, bringing its share of joys. Ed and Connie wrote of the arrival of their second daughter, and Len called to announce that Nora had given birth to another girl. Little Joy Ann wouldn't replace Shirley Emma, of course, but she did bring the happiness her name implied.

When Roy started talking about a new car in June, Emma said that the old model T would run a long while yet. She hated to see him spend all his lumber camp money on a car. But one Sunday morning in July, it refused to start. Sitting in that hot, dusty old rig with its flopping side curtains, watching the boys probe its innards, she realized that Roy was right.

She could hear the church bell ringing. If there was anything she hated, it was being late for church.

A few weeks later, Roy drove in with a brand new Overland. "Ka-OO-ga! Ka-OO-ga!" He blew the horn all the way into the yard, and the others came rushing out.

"It is nice," Emma said, as she climbed in and pulled Jeanie up beside her She stroked the gray plushy seat covers and rolled down the window.

Roy poked his head in the other window and grinned. "No more leaky roof, Ma!"

"And no more floppy old side curtains."

Carl and Henny immediately folded back the hood and put their heads deep into its motor, but Emma got out and admired the shiny chrome and deep blue paint.

Roy laid the bill down on the table when he came in for supper.

"Six hundred and forty dollars!" Emma exclaimed.

Carl whistled. "Good deal!"

"Sounds like an awful lot of money to me," Emma said, setting the pot roast on the table. She shook her finger at the boys. "Now we have no excuse. We'll get to church on time!"

There was a new spring in Roy's step since he got the car, Emma noticed, and it seemed like that car was always going out the driveway. Where those boys found the energy to go swimming at Pearson's lake or to play ball after a hard day's work, she didn't know. But it was good to see them laugh and banter, slick back their hair, and take off again. Winter would come soon enough, and they'd be housebound.

"I wonder if Ed will get down to see Jeanie before winter," Emma said one fall day. Sure enough, a few days later, he appeared.

He told them about John and Esther's new baby girl, Jean. John was about as proud as a father could be, according to Ed, but when Emma asked about Esther, he shook his head.

"Don't understand that woman. She says she's never going to have another baby. From what I hear, she didn't have an unusually difficult time. . . ."

After he left, Emma phoned Gertie. "I felt so sorry for Ed," she told her. Jeanie wouldn't go near him."

"Did she sing for him?"

"Oh, yes. She sat in the rocker and sang 'Let Me Call You Sweetheart' all the way through. And you know how the boys have taught her the names of all the cars. They say, 'What kinds of cars does your Daddy sell?' and she reels off the whole list, from Chevy to Whippet. Ed got a real kick out of that."

Emma had heard that Ed was seeing Amanda, his childhood sweetheart. It would be hard to see someone take Emmie's place, but she didn't blame Ed. His life must be pretty lonely.

Soon autumn turned to winter. A few weeks before Christmas, Emma was at Ella's when the children came home from practicing for the church program.

Harold gave Emma a slip of paper with a recitation written on it.

"We told Mrs. Semrow how good Jeanie can talk and asked if she could have a part. Mrs. Semrow said sure she can!"

"Oh, Harold. I'm not sure. She's only three."

"We'll teach her, Gramma!"

Before they went home, Jeanie could say the whole thing:

It's sweet to know that Jesus

Was once a baby, too.
We're trying to be like Him,
Loving and pure and true.

On Christmas Eve, Emma dressed Jeanie in new pink sateen bloomers, the red velveteen dress Ed had sent, and patent leather shoes which she shined with petroleum jelly. Emma was sure she was more nervous than Jeanie. Would she really speak in front of everybody?

It was a crisp, cold, starlit night with a few fast flying clouds. Carl carried Jeanie into church, and she pointed to the moon. "Moon's going fast."

Carl laughed. "No. The clouds are going fast."

Jeanie shook her head. "Uh-uh! The moon's going fast."

Carl grinned at Emma and shrugged. "Oh, well . . ."

When Jeanie's recitation was announced, Emma whispered, "Now, go way up the steps."

Jeanie's little legs were too short to walk up, so she climbed, using her hands and exposing a lot of pink bloomer. As she climbed, she said her recitation, and by the time she got to the top and turned around, she was all done!

She blinked her eyes, drew her little shoulders up, and put her hands over her mouth as if to say, "Now what do I do?"

Mrs. Semrow whispered, "Say it again."

Jeanie whispered back, loudly enough to be heard in the back row, "I did already!"

Emma beckoned to her, and she climbed down, the way she had climbed up, and ran to Emma's arms.

Emma smiled, but she couldn't help thinking, *If only Emmie were here to see her.*

How many more times she would feel that way in the years to come—at all the school and church programs. . . graduation from high school . . . at Jeanie's wedding. . . . Or would others be thinking, *if only Grandma could see her?*

Eleven

Changes in Store

E mma and Clara lingered at the table after dinner New Year's Day. "I can't get over how good you look," Clara said, smiling at Emma.

Emma refilled their coffee cups. "I really feel like me again," she answered.

She set the pot back on the stove and inched her chair a bit closer to her sister-in-law, so they could hear each other over the menfolk's loud talking from the next room.

"You know, I think I feel younger now than I did at fifty."

"And no wonder! Those were awfully hard years, when Al was sick. Took a lot out of you."

Jeanie toddled in and climbed up onto Clara's lap. Emma poured more milk in her blue enameled cup with the Dutch boy on the side. Then she stirred sugar into her coffee.

"Spoon. Spoon!" Jeanie demanded.

Clara laughed. "Monkey see, monkey do." She handed Jeanie a teaspoon.

Emma said, "But no sugar in milk, *Liebchen*. You can have a molasses cookie."

Jean munched a few minutes and then ran off to see what the men were doing.

"My, she's getting big," Clara observed.

Emma smiled. "Oh, yes. Says nursery rhymes and sings more songs than I can count, and she isn't even three. But there's so many years yet to go. . . ."

"Must be much easier for you this winter, with Roy home."

"We have enough stock now, that he felt he needed to be here. He's doing some logging right on our own place, too. Makes a world of difference to have him here.

"Henny, now, he'd sit down there day in and day out, in that little shack he built down in the timber. I hate having him down there alone, but he says it beats hiking an extra eight miles every day. Can't blame him."

"Does Carl get home weekends?

"Usually. He's in a camp way down near Merrill." Emma reached for a cookie. "I sure do miss him. He always has something to talk about. Roy is more quiet—wrapped up in his own thoughts most of the time."

"Children are all so different. Max is my companion. Don't know what I'd do without that boy."

The women looked toward the next room, where Max was down on his hands and knees, with Jeanie clinging to his back as he played bucking bronco.

"He'll get his knees all dirty. Look what they tracked in today! Need a new linoleum here in the kitchen. I'd like something besides brown and beige for a change—green, maybe."

"Isn't it nice the way they're making things more colorful? We need color—especially in winter."

"Colors do cheer a person up. I saw some material with yellow daisies—think that would look nice for curtains here?"

Clara nodded. "You're sure full of plans."

Emma smiled. "Seems so long since I had time to even look around and see what this place looks like. It's much easier now, with Jeanie trained. Right now I feel like I could go on and on like this—keeping house for the three of us, and doing for the other two whenever they come home."

One day in February, Roy sat at the kitchen table scribbling figures with a short pencil. "The cream check should look pretty good by spring," he told Emma. "Six more calves, and all the cows will be fresh."

"I was thinking," Emma said, scratching a pile of dirt across the worn linoleum with a stubby broom, "it would be nice to have a new linoleum and some new curtains." She glanced sideways at him as she swept the dirt into the heavy black dustpan.

"We'll see," he said, frowning.

Oh, well. Couldn't expect a man to get excited about a new floor and curtains. She'd mention it again in the spring.

As more cows freshened, Emma began helping with milking in the evening, unless it was stormy and Roy told her not to come to the barn. It was a pleasant diversion for Jeanie, too, especially when the lambs came.

Emma showed her how to find clover in the hay to feed the ewes. "Clover makes nice rich milk for the babies," she explained.

Jeanie held clumps of clover and giggled when the ewes nibbled it from her hands. She got exasperated with the lambs, who wouldn't come close enough to the side of the pen for her to pet them.

"Be patient," Roy would tell her. "When I'm done milking, I'll take one out and let you pet it."

He enjoyed taking a few minutes to watch her talk to the lamb and pet its soft baby-wool. Once Emma put a clean apron on Jeanie and hastily brushed her hair, so Roy could take a picture of her with a "sheepie."

"The way she loves animals, she ought to make a good farmer's wife," Emma remarked.

But it wasn't easy for Jeanie to understand shearing time. With Carl gone, Emma volunteered to help—but she hadn't counted on Jeanie's reaction. Each time she saw a struggling sheep or the shears gave one a little nick, Jeanie cried and begged them not to hurt the sheep.

"Honey, it's all right!" Emma tried to tell her "See. . . we put salve on them, and the hurt will go away. They're just scared when they kick and roll around. They aren't hurt."

Shearing sheep had never been Emma's favorite task, and this year it was exhausting. When the last one ran off, its head looking oddly large for its body, she heaved a huge sigh. "That's it for this year."

She took Jeanie's hand, and they walked down near the pasture fence. "See, they're fine. They had to get their wool off, or they'd be hot in summer."

They watched the lambs hunting for their mothers, bleating, "Baaa, baaa." The mothers answered with their deep "Baaas," until each lamb was matched with its own mother and blissfully nursing.

Emma went along to Merrill when Roy took the wool to the woolen mill and picked out yarn and a quilt bat. Then she and Jeanie went to the dime store, while Roy went to the hardware.

Jeanie stood wide-eyed and watched the little cans whisk back and forth on cables from the salesgirls to the cashier high in one corner of the store. Emma bought needles, bias tape, and peppermint candy.

They were hardly out of town before Jeanie was sound asleep, cuddled against Emma's plush coat.

"Those little eyes took in an awful lot today," Emma said.

It seemed a shame to wake her when they got to Tomahawk, but they had to stop at the A & P. Roy carried Jeanie in, and she perked up when she smelled the freshly ground coffee and heard Emma and Roy chatting with the white-aproned salesgirls. She giggled when they used the long stick with big grippers on it to pull down a box of corn flakes.

Roy carried out a fifty-pound sack of flour on his shoulder and came back for the box of groceries. "What kind of candy did they give us?" he asked.

"Chocolate drops."

"Ugh. Too sweet. Save 'em for Carl."

Emma never traveled the stretch of road between home and Tomahawk without thinking of all the trips Papa had made with the horses, taking butter and other products into town to sell.

"Used to take Papa all day just to do the trip to Tomahawk," she mused, knowing that Roy was following her thinking. "And here we've gone clear to Merrill and back in half a day—comfortable as can be, all closed in like this."

Roy is certainly enjoying this car, she thought. He had managed to go out at least one evening a week all winter. Even in heavy snow, he just put chains on, and away he went. Emma never asked him where he was going, but she knew he was involved with the young people in Ogema.

Thank goodness, he wasn't going to dance halls as he had a few years ago. She had never been concerned that drinking would be a problem for him, as it was for John, but she hated dance halls and anything connected with drinking. Drink had brought much unhappiness in her home when she was a child.

She worried some about Carl—and she didn't even want to think about what Henny would do, once he had a car and went on his own.

The fires had gone out when they got home. Before they took off their coats, Emma started the fire in the cookstove while Roy started the heater-stove. She tucked Jeanie in the rocker with the old brown blanket and gave her a graham cracker while she started supper.

Did me good to get out, she thought that night, as scenes of the day flickered before her mind's eye. I almost forget there's a big, old world out there. She thought of all the fine homes with electric lights and bathrooms, and wondered if their occupants could possibly be as content as she was.

One evening in March Emma brought out the catalog and found the linoleum she had admired. She waited until Roy turned a page of the paper and then slid the catalog across the table to him.

"How do you like this for the kitchen?"

"Hmm. Don't think you better plan on it right now."

Emma pulled the catalog back. "Oh, that's all right. If you don't think we can afford it. . . . There's no hurry." She put the catalog back on the shelf.

"No, that's not it," Roy said, frowning and biting his lower lip. "Ma, come sit down. I've got something to tell you."

Emma sat down. "Now don't you worry. I'm used to waiting for things. That doesn't bother me."

He shook his head and took a deep breath. "Ma. Helen and I are getting married."

"Married!" Her hands fell in her lap.

Roy nodded.

"But I don't even know this, this Helen."

"But I do. Oh, Ma, she's one special girl." His eyes lit up as he continued. "Never met a girl like her before. She's not just a pretty girl with nothing upstairs. She thinks. She's got definite opinions, and she reads and learns. You remember when I brought her home one Sunday last fall? Carl and Lou Ella Anderson were with us."

"Hmm. Real dark hair, brown eyes?"

"Uh huh."

"Not overly friendly, I remember."

"She's shy, Ma. But not with me. We talk and talk."

"Pretty, that I remember."

Roy beamed.

"But where on earth are you going to live?"

"Well, that's what I want to talk to you about. We were thinking that if we moved your cook-stove to the front room—"

"My cook-stove in the front room!" Her voice rose.

Roy held up his hand. "Hold on now, Ma! It's right next to your bedroom and big enough for this table—with the leaves out—and a couple chairs and your rocker and the one Hank likes. And we'll get you a cupboard for your dishes. . . ."

Emma shook her head and covered her face with her hands. "No . . . no. I can't talk about it now." She was crying too hard to continue.

Roy came around the table and put his hands gently on her shoulders. "I'm sorry, Ma. We'll work something out. But we are getting married."

The next day Emma moved about in a daze. Everything she saw and used—her beloved east window, her convenient flour bin, all the spacious pantry shelves, the pump right outside the door, her sink—all anchored her to her present way of life.

At bed time she tried to pray, but all she could get out was, "Father, help me!"

The next day was worse. She stopped in the front room doorway and tried to imagine being shut in that room with only the north and east window—both darkened by the porch. And no sink drain!

"At my age, I should start carrying a slop pail again!" she grumbled.

She thought about telling the girls how she felt, but she certainly couldn't do it over the phone—not unless she wanted to take a chance that no one on the thirteen-party line would be listening. Besides, young folks stick together, and everyone loves lovers. Fine chance she'd have of getting them to understand how she felt.

At noon she caught Roy studying her solicitously, but she went about her work as though nothing had changed. It wasn't easy to ignore her throbbing headache, especially when Jeanie decided this was the day she wanted to plink and plunk on the piano. Over and over Emma distracted her to quieter play, but her high little voice cut through Emma's ears no matter what she did.

When Jeanie was finally down for a nap, Emma heated the coffee and poured herself a cup, her thoughts churning. She hadn't even asked Roy when they planned to get married.

She finished her coffee and went to water the plants in the bay window. The bay window! What on earth would she do with the big carnation she took in each fall, and all her geraniums and the Christmas cactus she'd had since she couldn't remember when. And the fuschia and the wandering Jew and the huge Boston fern on the pedestal. She began to cry, quietly at first; then, when she was way back in the pantry, she let the sobs roll out.

Eventually she fished a hanky out of her apron pocket and mopped her face. "Got to get a hold of myself," she said out loud. "Ain't the end of the world!"

But when Jeanie woke up crying and crabby, Emma felt like crying all over again. "I'm supposed to take care of this little one like a young woman, but now I'm supposed to sit in a couple little rooms like an old lady," she sputtered.

That night she put off getting Jeanie to bed, so she wouldn't have to talk with Roy. But he was sitting by the table, as usual, when she came out of the bedroom. She picked up her knitting without a word.

Roy cleared his throat several times and finally said, "Forgot to tell you. We set the date for October first. Figured that'd be a good time. Fall work'll be done and the weather still nice." Emma swallowed and nodded. She couldn't answer. Tears were too close.

She felt a bit relieved the next day, knowing there was still six months before the wedding. A lot of water will run downhill by that time, she told herself. But by evening, tension tightened its grip on her and her head ached again.

"I've got a headache," she told Roy after Jeanie was down. "I'm going to bed."

"Sleep good, Ma," he said gently.

Ella and Gertie both called the next day, wondering why they hadn't heard from her. She didn't let on that she was troubled, and they didn't mention anything about the engagement. Roy evidently hadn't told anyone else.

If only she could talk to Clara, but she didn't want to ask Roy to take her visiting. She didn't want to ask him for anything right now.

Her opportunity came a few days later, when Roy said he had to go to Phillips. He wondered if she'd like to ride along to visit Nora or go as far as Ogema to visit Gertie or Minnie.

When Roy dropped her off at Clara's, Emma didn't have any idea how she was going to tell Clara the news. They exchanged small-talk for awhile. But when Max took Jeanie to see the kittens, Emma said, "Clara, Roy's getting married!" and promptly burst into tears.

Clara sat down, dish towel in hand "Why, Emma! Don't you like the girl? Who is she?"

"I don't even know her. Saw her a couple times. Her name is Helen. Helen Risberg. You know, the carpenter's daughter. He died a couple years ago."

"I don't know them, but I've heard they're a nice family."

Emma blew her nose. "It's just. . . ." She started to cry again. "I'm not ready. I don't want to be shoved off in a corner. I can't give up my house!"

"But where else could they live, Emma? You and Jeanie don't need all that room, and Carl and Hank aren't home much anymore."

"I know . . . but it ain't fair! I've got this little one to take care of like a young woman, and yet I'm being put out to pasture like an old mare! Roy thinks we should make the front room into a sort of living room kitchen combination, 'cause it's next to my bedroom."

"That room's nice and big."

"But my bay window and my sink and my pantry. . . ."

Max came in with Jeanie riding on his shoulders, and Emma hastily turned to help Clara set the table, hiding her red eyes.

Walter came in, washed his hands, and then pinched Jeanie's nose between two bent fingers. "I've got your nose!" he said, letting the tip of his thumb stick out between his fingers.

Jeanie patted her nose and shook her head. "Uh uh! It's still there!"

"Oh, no, it isn't," he said, showing her his thumb again.

Clara poked Walter in the ribs. "Stop that now!"

"Oh, don't worry," Emma said. She welcomed the diversion. "She knows he's only teasing."

"Hey, Auntie!" Max said, as he speared a fat slice of home baked bread. "Roy told me he's getting married in the fall. It'll be kinda nice for you to have a woman to talk with for a change, won't it?"

Emma smiled a weak smile, knowing Clara was shooting him warning looks.

But he went on. "That Helen—she sure is religious. Can't get Roy to go to dances or even have a beer anymore."

Emma's brows shot up. "So that's why he hasn't been going to dances."

Clara smiled, as if to say, "See, there's one more thing to be thankful for."

"Anyway, there's a few months yet," Emma said to

Clara as she dried dishes.

"Are you hoping they'll break up?"

"I don't know. Guess I've been thinking so much about myself, I haven't thought about them."

"Maybe when you've seen them together you'll feel better about the whole thing. Why don't you invite her over?"

"I hadn't even thought about that."

"She sounds like a nice girl. I always wanted to go up the Risberg hill, but I never had any reason to. Folks say it's a beautiful place—the winding road through the woods is so pretty and there's even a lake there."

When Emma was leaving, Clara put her hand on Emma's arm. "Emma, you care about that boy, don't you?"

Emma was so startled she couldn't even answer. On the way home she half listened as Roy told her about stopping at Len's. Of all things to ask her! Of course she cared about Roy. She loved him—and that wasn't a word she used easily or lightly.

She had expected Clara to be a little more sympathetic. Surely, even though she was eight years younger, she could put herself in Emma's shoes. What did she mean, "You care about that boy, don't you?"

By the next morning, Emma's indignation was boiling over. Care about him! Why, Clara should remember how Roy took over when Papa died. She should know how grateful Emma was for his dependability. And Clara surely knew how well they got along.

Emma sliced bread, muttering, "There isn't much I wouldn't do for that boy!"

Then she caught her breath and clapped her hand over her mouth. What had she said? Suddenly she felt light-headed and sat down, her thoughts whirling.

"Oh, Lord, I've done it again—got so tied up feeling sorry for myself, I couldn't see anything else."

She didn't feel like crying now. She felt stunned.

"Where do I start? Help me, Father!"

She hurried to her dresser and opened her Bible to the place where a little slip of paper stuck out. "Charity suffereth long, and is kind . . . seeketh not her own . . . is not easily prevoked . . . endureth all things. . . ."

"Forgive me, Father. I've been so selfish. Help me let go of it! I want to love like I'm supposed to."

Gently she laid the Bible down, leaned over close to the old spotted mirror, and said out loud, "Emma Verleger, you've got a lot of planning to do!"

Twelve

Young Love

The next day Emma had a lot of time to think while she ironed. *I'll think about Roy and Helen and get my mind off myself,* she resolved. *It's going to take some doing to feel happy about this change, but I'm willing to try.*

She set the iron back on the stove, detached the handle, and laid it on the gray speckled reservoir cover while she put more wood in the stove. Then she hung up a freshly ironed apron.

Helen. She tried to recall every detail of the girl. Certainly different from her brown-haired, blue-eyed daughters—not only was her hair dark brown—almost black—but it was bobbed! Emma couldn't picture Ella or Gertie or Minnie or any of the boys' wives with short hair. But times change. No reason why they shouldn't cut their hair, too, one of these days, instead of wearing it pulled severely back and secured in a pug.

She unrolled a bundle of sprinkled pillow cases and began to iron one that Emmie had embroidered for her. Helen would never know Emmie. Would she ever understand how loved she had been? Would she think less of her when she learned of Emmie's hasty wedding?

Roy said Helen played piano. It wouldn't be easy to have this dark-haired stranger play Emmie's piano, but she'd get used to it. Helen surely had the hands for it—long tapered fingers and lovely oval nails. Roy surely must be thrilled to hold those lovely hands. She looked down at her own square hands with their stubby, short-nailed fingers and sighed.

She turned the pillowcase over, pressed it hard to make the embroidery stand out, and carefully folded it, giving it a quick swipe with the iron after every fold. Suddenly she wanted to see Helen again. She wanted to see the two of them together.

That noon, after she had tucked Jeanie in for her nap, Emma stood with her arms folded and surveyed the front room. Something would have to be done about the arch—double doors put in, maybe. There was room for the cook-stove on that wall and, continuing clockwise, there'd be space for a bench for the water-pail to the left of her bedroom door. Then, to the right of it, the table and chairs would fit. She'd push the table against the wall to save space.

She studied the elaborate etched-glass door window—a stag with antlers her sons would prize. Too fancy for a kitchen, but then, that end would be the dining-living room end. She'd keep the wooden rocker right where it was. Henny liked that one. And the square walnut table with the scalloped edge and ball and claw feet could stay there in front of the north window.

She measured the remaining wall space with her eye. Her rocker could go by the east window, and the rest of the wall could be for a little wash stand with a mirror above it and a cupboard beside. She turned and walked out on the narrow porch with its railing all around it.

After supper that evening, she led Roy through the house and out the front door "Look here," she said, pointing to the railing at the end of the porch. "How about taking that section off, so I can carry my slop pail out this way. I can throw it out back of the lilac bush at the edge of the field."

His surprised expression gave way to sheer delight, and she had to blink back tears.

Roy peered over the end and said, "Pretty high. We better have Floyd build a step—a big wide one."

"I think I'll transplant a honeysuckle back here and make a flower bed along the house. Never did much with this end before," she rambled on, not wanting him to comment on her change of heart.

A little later she watched him stride down to the barn, whistling cheerfully. She wouldn't have been surprised had he suddenly jumped up and clicked his heels together. *What's an old sink drain compared to that boy's happiness*, she thought, as she poured the dish water down the drain.

Instead of his usual quick wash-up after chores, Roy mixed lather in his shaving cup and carefully frosted his face. He turned to Emma, brush in hand. "Everyone comin' over for your birthday Sunday?"

"'Most everybody, I guess. Gert says she's baking my cake."

"Good," he said, twisting his mouth to the left and scraping carefully with his safety razor. "Guess it's time to tell 'em the big news."

"How come you told Max the other day?"

Roy tilted his head toward the light and kept shaving. "Oh. . . . I guess I just hadda tell someone." He frowned. "I asked him not to tell anyone."

"Well, it's high time the family knew, or there'll be hurt feelings."

She heard him take the stairs two at a time, and when he came down with a crisp shirt and corduroy pants on, she said, "It's Thursday night. You going to see Helen?"

"Yup!" he said with a grin which mellowed to a gentle smile as he said, "Ma . . . thanks!" And he was gone.

On Sunday the men congregated in the dining room, the women in the kitchen, as usual. Emma waited for a break in the conversation, but when none came she broke in loudly, "Girls! We had a letter from Ed yesterday. Connie's going to have another baby in the fall."

"That'll be four already. . . ."

"So close together. . . ."

"Well, Ed's a lot of help around the house."

Ella piped up. "I've got an announcement, too. I'm going to have a baby in October!"

Then there were exclamations!

"I thought Gracie would be my last," she continued. "After all, I'll be thirty-seven."

"Oh, for goodnes sake," Emma said. "You could have a couple more yet. I was forty-one when Hank was born."

"Oh, Ma! Don't say that! Seven is enough!"

They were laughing and talking so loudly they didn't even hear the car drive in. When Emma turned to get the coffee pot, there stood Roy in the doorway—with Helen standing shyly at his side.

"Ah-HEM!" he said. "I'd like you to meet Helen Risberg—soon to be Helen Verleger. Helen, you've met my mother. This is my sister Ella, and my sister Gertie, and Mamie, Al's wife, and my sister Minnie. . ."

"Congratulations!

"When's the wedding?"

"So happy to meet you, Helen."

The men came to see what all the commotion was about, and there were more introductions. Helen didn't cling to Roy physically, but her eyes pleaded, "Please don't leave me!" They didn't stay long; they were off to tell the news to Helen's family.

After the couple had left, all eyes turned to Emma.

Ella asked the question: "Where are they going to live?" Emma was able to tell them all about the plans and not even feel like crying.

That night, at bedtime, she whispered, "Lord, you are so good! You worked it all out. A week ago I could have just bawled, but now I can talk about the plans like they were my idea in the first place. But Father, when things get rough, please help me remember how those two look at each other."

In May Emma's thoughts went beyond her own little world as she tried to imagine how Charles Lindberg felt flying thirty-three hours across the Atlantic all by himself. It was all anyone talked about. Hank had cut out a picture of the crowd of nearly 100,000 people greeting Lindberg at an airport near Paris, and tacked it up in his room.

"My goodness!" Emma exclaimed one afternoon. "What would Papa say? Who ever thought anyone would fly across the Atlantic ocean?"

"Al says there'll be aeroplanes big enough to carry a hundred people some day," Hank said.

Emma chuckled. "Sounds like Al. Maybe it will happen, but I don't think I'll live to see it."

Another thing Lindberg's flight did was to give the youngsters a new hero. At the Fourth of July picnic the little boys—arms outstretched—playing aeroplane all afternoon.

Roy brought Helen to the picnic for awhile; then they went to be with her family. She still said very little—just smiled a lot.

"Oh, to be young and in love. . . ." Gertie sighed, as they drove off with enough space in the front seat for another passenger.

Often that summer, Emma and Jeanie would be sitting on the porch swing when Roy drove out in his shiny blue Overland. There were always peonies, roses, or whatever happened to be in bloom nodding in the crystal vases mounted inside the car on the post between the windows.

The dialogue was always the same.

"Where's Roy goin'?" Jeanie would ask.

"To see Helen."

"Always goin' ta see Helen," the little girl would pout.

"That's 'cause they're going to get married."

"I wanna get married, too!"

"Not for a year or two, *Liebchen*."

Then Emma would sing to Jeanie and dream a bit. She'd imagine Roy and Helen doing all those young-parent things with Jeanie that Emma's stiffening joints prevented her from doing—splashing and running in the lake, coasting on the crust in winter—things like that.

She wanted to share those dreams with Jeanie, but she kept singing instead. She'd not make promises that weren't hers to keep. She certainly didn't intend to foist the responsibility for Jeanie's care onto the young couple—not as long as she was able to care for the child herself. But supposing there should come a time she wasn't able. . . .

The day before the threshers were due, Roy said, "Well, Ma, next year Helen'll take over. She'll need your help, but you won't have the full responsibility."

And so Emma faced the threshing dinner with a blend of nostalgia and relief. By nightfall, as she hung up the dishpan and crept off to bed bone-weary, her mood was definitely one of relief.

One Sunday before the wedding, Helen's mother invited Emma and Jeanie for dinner. They spent a pleasant afternoon with Mrs. Risberg, a quiet-spoken little lady who appeared to be in no rush about anything, and Helen's sister and her family. It was reassuring to meet the people who would come to visit and become a part of their lives.

Emma had hoped the house could be reorganized before the wedding, but it didn't work out that way. Helen and Roy were too busy with wedding and honeymoon arrangements. Nest-building would come later.

The first day of October dawned clear and warm. Emma inspected Roy's and Carl's suits that she had painstakingly pressed the day before. Carl and Lou Ella would be the attendants.

Emma and Jeanie rode to Ogema with Carl in his little Ford coupe early enough to spend a few minutes at Gertie's before the wedding. They found Ed, Jeanie's dad, there also—with his friend, Amanda. He coaxed Jeanie over to him by showing her the picture of her and the lamb he carried in his wallet, and she did sit on his lap a few minutes.

When they left for the wedding, Ed took Emma's arm and apologized for not visiting for such a long while.

"That's all right," she told him. "You have your own life." What she wanted to say was, "We can make without you."

In church Emma was too preoccupied keeping Jeanie quiet to think sentimental thoughts, but when the organ music began, her throat tightened. She looked up at Roy and Carl and realized they were no longer "boys" but grown men.

When the organ announced the bride's entrance, necks craned—but Emma couldn't tear her gaze from the tender glow in Roy's blue eyes as he watched his bride come down the aisle.

My! She was beautiful and radiant—and aware only of Roy, it seemed.

"Oh, Father, keep them always devoted to each other—long after this first love-bloom fades," Emma prayed.

Though Emma talked and laughed with family and friends at the reception in the church basement, her throat still ached. When the young couple ran through a shower of rice to Roy's car, she let a little sob escape.

The next morning she woke feeling she had been

abandoned. She dreaded going to church and answering questions. She wished instead she could wander down to the old house, cry awhile, and sort out her feelings, but she climbed into Carl's little car, determined to keep her feelings under control.

"You look awfully tired, Ma," Ella said after church. "Better take a nap this afternoon."

"I might," she answered, but she was still thinking about taking that walk.

When Jeanie went down for her nap, Emma saw her opportunity. Leaving Carl stretched out on the couch with an ear open for Jeanie, she cut across the field and over to the stone piles where she and Jeanie had picked spring flowers, then up through the pasture and across another field to the site of the old house.

There was nothing but a rectangle of stones and high weeds now. Too bad they couldn't somehow have preserved it. She tore off some dry grass around the flat stone that had served as the doorstep and sat down. Hugging her knees, she studied the landscape to the north—the house, barn, tool shed and the trees tucked in between the buildings. Then she turned to the south and the river.

Twenty-five years since they had left the little house, but it seemed like yesterday that she was hanging out clothes, watching Al tear out stumps and plow those first little fields. They'd stand at twilight looking over the newly cleared section, basking in the elation of accomplishment, and Al would tell her his latest plans.

He was always the one to plan, while she hung back with more of a let's-wait-and-see attitude. It was when he stopped making plans that she knew he had given up hope of living. The pain grew worse and worse, and when the doctor operated and simply closed him back up, she knew only a miracle would save him—and miracles were scarce these days.

Suddenly she realized that Helen would never know

Al. How would this shy girl have coped with his teasing, she wondered. How she wished he could know all that had gone on. It wasn't right to try to talk to dead people, was it?

"Lord, will you tell him? Tell him how well Roy has done, and that Carl is going to be a fine young man, and Henny—just tell him he's a real trapper—like my brother, Fred. Oh, and tell him . . . tell him . . . I miss him."

A torrent of sobs rolled out into the quiet. They came and came until she wondered if there was an end to them. Then, when they subsided and she had dried her eyes, she walked up into the woods through the autumn leaves.

Why, she wondered, as she strolled along through the rustling leaves, *doesn't a person notice how black tree limbs are when the leaves are green? Surely they don't suddenly turn darker as the leaves turn color.* Now they stood in stark contrast to the countless shades of gold and red.

A moss-covered log invited her to sit down. "Father, I don't understand. Why do I feel so empty? I want to cry everytime I see the way those young folks look at each other. Am I jealous? I guess I am, in a way. Al never did look at me like that. Things were sort of matter-of-fact. Oh, you know we loved each other. We had a good marriage—but there wasn't that special something I see between these two.

"Oh, but I'm not yearning for another man! Goodness, no! I've got all I can handle right now! It's just . . . I guess I'm love-hungry. Lord, I know you love me, but I don't feel our love. I sure do feel love for you. It's been there ever since I was a little girl and my uncle called me the "little heathen" because I hadn't been baptized. And one day in that little church in Oshkosh, I told you I didn't want to be 'no heathen'—that I wanted to belong to You all the rest of my life and be with you for all eternity. But then, why do I feel like this?"

Again she started to cry, looking up at the black branches, brilliant leaves, and blue sky, until tears ran down her cheeks and on down her neck.

"Jesus . . . Jesus . . . I feel so empty."

Something was happening. Something that had never happened to her before. She didn't breathe. She didn't move—except to close her eyes. What was it? Something soft, warm, falling all over her, but not only on her but in her, permeating every cell of her body. It was like being held with infinite tenderness. "Oh, Jesus," she breathed. "It's You. It's You. Oh, thank you, thank you."

Tears ran unheeded. "I love You, I trust You."

Oh, if I could stay like this forever, she thought. But that special, indescribable something was going, going, gone, leaving a peace she had never experienced before and a new joy glowing deep within her.

"Oh, my," she said out loud. "I never imagined there could be anything like this. Lord, you're so good to me! I don't deserve it!"

How long had she been here? She had lost all sense of time. She'd better hurry home.

Back through the dry leaves she rustled, and through the fence. Scarcely glancing at the old house site, Emma hurried toward home—each step a thank you.

What had happened? She didn't know, but one thing she knew; that empty feeling was completely gone!

Roy had said they would be home by Monday. A whole week ahead of her, and all she could do was keep up the regular work and try not to be too curious about the various crates that stood in the tool shed.

She did investigate the ivory and blue stove, running her hand over the shiny enamel of the warming oven. Who ever dreamed of a colored stove? She peeked at a corner of the roll of linoleum for the kitchen—blue, to match the stove—as well as the one for her room—the green one that she had looked at for so long.

She went out shaking her head. These young folks, did they appreciate all these new things? She and Al had been content with home made and hand-me-downs. But why shouldn't they have new things, if they could afford it? Young people should have pretty new things.

The week dragged, and the boys were unusually quiet.

One night at supper time Emma said, "You'd think we've just had a funeral around here, not a wedding."

"Sure is going to be different around here," muttered Hank.

Carl agreed. "Won't ever be the same."

She hadn't even thought how the boys would be affected by the change.

The night Helen and Roy came home, Emma didn't even hear them, but her heart lurched when she saw Roy's car in the yard in the morning.

He didn't get up for chores, and she tried to keep Jeanie quiet for awhile. Around eight she gave up and let her play the piano.

She stopped abruptly when the stair door opened. Roy and Helen stood in the doorway, hand in hand. Jeanie dashed to Roy, and he tossed her up in the air.

Emma watched them and laughed, but when she looked at Helen her laughter stopped. Helen was watching, too. But she wasn't smiling.

Thirteen

Henny

The day Roy and Helen came home things began to hum. Carl had decided to stay home and work with Roy in the woods for a few months, and Hank hadn't started trapping, so that week the three of them laid the linoleum in the front room, moved Emma's stove in, and helped Floyd, the carpenter, install the double doors and build the porch step.

Helen's kitchen floor was laid next, and the bright blue and ivory stove set up. Meanwhile she painted a drop-leaf table and four chairs blue and ivory to match the stove. She even painted a little bottle blue to use for a vase.

"I'd never have thought of doing that," Emma told her.

It wasn't an easy week for Jeanie, who had an exceptional talent for being right where someone wanted to move. She played a long while with the new door knobs—glass with a star design deep inside.

"Mama, look! Aren't they beautiful?"

"She calls me 'Mama'," Emma explained to Helen, "but she knows I'm her grandmother. The pictures of Emmie and Ed have helped me explain things to her."

Sunday came fast that week. As Emma dressed for church she wondered how many people were curious about Roy's bride. Not all of them had been at the wedding.

Roy began introducing her as they went up the church steps, but when Mr. Zielkie began ringing the bell, they all hurried in.

Emma took her usual seat on the women's side, but to her astonishment, Helen went with Roy to the men's side! Roy didn't look a bit perturbed.

Not daring to look around to see the reactions, Emma stared at her toes as her cheeks grew warm. *Well, it's time we broke that tradition,* she thought, remembering how when Fred was home she had wanted to sit with her boys.

She said as much to several of the women after church, and they politely agreed—but she was quite certain that the incident would be the table topic in many homes that noon. On the way home, she let Helen know her feelings . . . but she realized that it really didn't matter to Helen what Emma or anyone else thought. She was a woman of strong convictions and acted on them.

Once the furniture was moved, Emma set about completing the details of her compact home. The ecru, tatting-edged curtains Gertie had made years ago, that had once appeared so elegant, now hung limp and dreary. She hung fluffy, dotted white Priscillas in their place.

The little glass-doored cupboard Roy had bought posed another problem. It had been designed to display attractive pieces, not Emma's hodge-podge of dishes and groceries. White gathered curtains hung on the inside of the doors hid its modest contents.

One evening, after Jeanie was tucked in, Emma sat down with a sigh. So far she certainly hadn't felt shoved in a corner—not with Carl and Hank still to cook and wash for. In fact, she wished she weren't quite so busy, so she could go and help Ella a little after the baby came.

If only she lived closer to Ed and Connie and their four little ones. Those two certainly had their hands full.

A week later Roy poked his head in the door and said, "Ella's Hank just called. She had a baby boy!"

The next day he took Emma over to see little James Alton. Ella was doing well, but Jeanie's clamoring to see the baby and hold him was making her nervous, so they didn't stay long. They stopped to see Gertie on their way home.

"How are things working out with you and Helen?" she asked when they stopped by after visiting Ella.

"Just fine!" Emma could answer honestly. "She says there's no reason why my plants can't stay in the bay window, though I don't think she's fond of that big fern. And she says I should go ahead and wash on Mondays, 'cause she knows I always like to get the washing out of the way the first of the week. We'll both use the sewing machine; I can move it in to my rooms when I want to.

"It really is nice to have a woman to talk with. Sometimes we get going and talk for a whole hour."

"I'm glad, Ma. It isn't easy for two women to be under the same roof. They both have to be generous."

Later, when Emma was alone, she thought, *Yes, Helen's generous all right—with everything except Roy.*

One night Jeanie ran into their kitchen after supper and crawled up on Roy's lap. Helen ushered her back into Emma's room and shut the door firmly behind her.

Little Jeanie cried as Emma rocked her. She didn't understand why she had been banished, but Emma did. It wasn't easy, she knew, to have an old lady and a little child always around when you're a newly-wed.

She also knew she had been foolish to dream as she had. Helen was not nearly as delighted with Jeanie as the rest of the family. She considered her spoiled and, probably, if the truth were known, a nuisance.

"Ah, she's young," Emma said to herself. "Right now her heart can't hold more than her family and Roy. It will grow in time. But will it grow enough soon enough?"

In November one of Hank's dreams came true when he found a young hound for sale. He named the dog Sport.

"He's a small hound," Hank assured Emma. "He won't eat much."

Emma patted his sleek head. "Seems like a nice dog. We'll feed him by my door and hope he doesn't bother Colonel."

It was a prayer answered for Emma, also. Now Henny wouldn't be alone out there in the woods.

Christmas was the liveliest in years, with Helen and Roy's guests coming and going. Jeanie had a recitation again, and this time she turned completely around before she spoke.

Al made her a little doll crib, and Emma made tiny sheets and a puffy comforter. Jeanie was delighted when she saw it under the tree.

Ed sent two little dresses, but he didn't come to see her.

"Just as well," Emma said when Jeanie couldn't hear her.

But the nicest part of Christmas was Helen playing Christmas carols on the piano.

New Year's Eve Emma was alone again, but she didn't mind at all. There were even more family members to pray for this year—not that she didn't pray for them all year long.

As she put wood in the three stoves before bed, she thought of all the changes the year had brought. She couldn't even have imagined them when she'd sat and thought and prayed last New Year's Eve. It hadn't all been easy to accept, but she was content.

Content, but never free of concern for Jeanie. So many more years to go before she'd be on her own. . . .

Though Emma felt less anxious about Henny, now that he had Sport, she still looked forward to his coming home after he had been gone a few days. One Wednesday, in February, as she cut up wilting carrots for stew, she was expecting to see his silhouette against the white snow about dusk. She always saw a dark spot bobbing along and then, at the top of the hill, the rest of him would come into view.

"Henny comin' home?" Jeanie asked, sensing her anticipation.

"Yes. Henny's coming home," Emma assured her.

She stole several quick glances up the road before dusk, but kept busy cutting carpet strips and sewing them together. She had taught Jeanie how to wind the long, multicolored strip on a ball. Jeanie waited, none too patiently, in her little green rocker, until the strip was several yards long; then she eagerly wound it up.

At five Emma put her hand work away and set the table for the four of them. Surely he'd come soon.

Carl came in, cold and hungry. Emma lit the lamp and dished up the stew.

"Henny should be coming any minute," she said when they sat down.

But he still wasn't there when they had finished eating and Carl had gone to help with chores. Ears tuned to Henny's step on the porch, Emma washed dishes.

"Mama? When's Henny comin?" Jeanie asked about every five minutes.

Finally Emma snapped, "I don't know when he's coming! You just wait!"

When dishes were done, Jeanie ran to get the tattered gray Bible story book and snuggled up on Emma's lap.

"Well, now, let's see. We read about Noah, and about Abraham and Isaac. . . ."

"Lions! Read about the lions!"

"Daniel in the lions' den. All right."

Emma read the story and made an excuse to put wood in the stove so she could take a peek out the window. It was too dark to see up the hill now, so she sat back down and read another of Jeanie's favorites—Moses in the basket.

At seven-thirty she washed Jeanie's hands and face and helped her into her long flannel nighty. Then she wrapped a blanket around her and sat down and sang to her awhile—but her mind was on her young trapper.

Jeanie didn't want to go to bed until she saw Henny, but Emma told her she'd see him in the morning.

"Henny didn't come home last night like he said he would," she told Carl the next morning. "He only took enough food to last three days. I'm worried."

"Aw, he's all right. He'll cook a rabbit if he gets hungry."

"He could have fallen or something. . . ."

"He'll be home tonight," Carl assured her as he strode off to do chores.

That evening it was doubly hard to keep her eyes off the window. Jeanie's constant questions didn't help.

At six, when Carl came, they ate supper. Again Emma washed the dishes and read to Jeanie. Her mouth said the words, but her mind was in prayer, as it had been most of the day.

Suddenly Jeanie popped up. "Sport's out there!"

Emma all but dumped her off her lap as she rushed to the door. There he was, scratching at the door and whining.

"Well! You beat Henny home, did you? I bet you're hungry." She put some scraps in his dish and watched him wolf them down. "You are hungry," she said as she went to get more.

Emma heated the left-over pot-roast and peered out the window. But strain as she would, she couldn't see a bit of movement on the hillside. Maybe he was coming up the hill out of her range of vision. She waited, trying to ignore Jeanie's clamoring.

She opened the door and listened. Sport jumped up, tail wagging eagerly. "Where is he, boy? Oh, I wish you could talk! Is he hurt?"

"Henny hurt? Jeanie asked.

"No, no. I was just talking to Sport. Henny's all right."

Roy and Carl were still doing chores, but she went to talk with Helen. "I'm really worried now. Sport came home alone."

Helen murmured something about Henny's being old enough to take care of himself, and Emma went back to her room thinking that Helen would have to have children of her own before she could understand.

She had Jeanie in bed by the time Roy and Carl finished chores. When she heard them come in, she hurried to confront them.

"Henny isn't home yet, and I know something has happened to him." She burst into tears and pulled up her apron to hide her face.

"He'll be home tomorrow," Roy said assuringly.

And Carl said, "Aw, Ma. Don't worry."

She gave her face a quick mop and shook her finger at them. "I want you to go down there and find him! Now! Tonight."

Roy talked over his shoulder as he washed his hands. "Ma, it's eight o'clock!"

"You can be down there in an hour, can't you?"

Carl shrugged. "Take longer than that in the dark." He shot a questioning glance at Roy.

Roy dried his hands, frowning. "Oh, all right." He shook his head. "It is funny that the dog came home."

"We better take two lanterns," Carl said.

Emma brought them in from the porch and filled them with kerosene.

Helen didn't say a word.

The boys would drive to the edge of the woods and then walk another two miles or so. *Good thing there hasn't been any fresh snow*, Emma thought. They'd be able to follow Henny's tracks.

After they left, she sagged into her rocker praying, "Lord, go with them. You know how I hate sending them out in the cold and the dark. Be with Henny. Let him know help is coming."

"Mama?" Jeanie called from her crib. "Henny home?"

"Not yet! Go to sleep now."

At nine Emma took down her hair and braided it. She leaned back, eyes closed. Suddenly she felt a little hand on her knee. There stood Jeanie, tears running down her cheeks.

Emma pulled her up on her lap. "What are you doing awake?"

"I want Henny," she sobbed.

"There, there. Carl and Roy went down to get him. You go to sleep now, and in the morning they'll all be here."

She put Jeanie back to bed and knit until her eyes got tired. At ten she undressed and put on her old flannel robe. She checked the fire and peeked in to see if Helen was still up, but she had gone to bed.

Each time she saw car lights she held her breath, hoping they'd turn in the driveway. Too restless to sit, she paced through the house.

"Oh, Lord, I wish I could stop my thoughts. I want to trust you, but I keep thinking of all the things that might have happened."

The clock struck eleven.

Emma put wood in all the stoves and started a fresh pot of coffee. They'd be cold when they got home.

Lights! Car lights! Down the hill—across the bridge, up the hill—into the driveway!

She hurried to Helen's kitchen window.

Henny came in first, dragging his heavy knapsack.

She wanted to throw her arms around him, but he brushed past her into their room. "Are you all right?" she called.

"He's all right," Roy said glumly.

Carl shook his head. "He was lyin' on his bunk readin' a cowboy magazine!"

"Didn't even want to come home with us," added Roy.

Emma didn't know what to say. She walked back to her room, where Henny was unlacing his snowpacks.

"Oh, Henny! I was so worried!"

"Oh, for Pete's sake, don't call me Henny! And don't worry about me."

"But I knew you didn't have food, and then Sport came home. . . ."

"Aw, I didn't feed him any of my bread the way I usually do. Kept it for myself, so I could stay longer. Thought he'd catch himself a rabbit if he got hungry."

Hank ate some bread and jelly and went to bed without another word.

Emma fell into bed wishing she could stay there for a week. "Father, help me! I'm so mixed up!"

Before her mind was making sense the next morning, Emma knew something was wrong. Then recollections rushed in pell mell. Henny was home—safe! But rude and self-centered as ever.

"Don't call me Henny!" She couldn't blame him. "Henny" did sound babyish.

Roy and Carl—how could she tell them how grateful she was? She had hated to insist that they go way down there in the dark, but she had to. Did they think she cared about Henny—Hank—more than she did for them?

Oh, how she wanted them to care about Hank and not be disgusted with him. He hadn't even wanted to come home with them! Had eaten the food meant for his dog! And Carl had heard him snap at her, too.

Wearily, she crept out of bed, tended the fire, and got dressed. She dreaded seeing Hank drag behind, late for chores again, but she couldn't rap on the ceiling to wake him up anymore—his bed was right above Helen's stove.

Only Jeanie's prattle broke the breakfast silence.

When they were done eating, Carl said, "You can help cut wood today, Hank."

"Got a lotta hides to stretch."

"They'll keep. We're low on wood."

Hank shuffled out behind him.

All forenoon, as Emma baked bread and cooked, she dug back into the past. What had she done wrong? She reviewed the list she knew so well:

She'd allowed Minnie and Gertie to pamper him.

She'd neglected him when Papa was sick.

She'd let him have his own way because it was easier than disciplining.

If only she had talked to him more when he was young. He must have been lonely when Minnie and Gertie got married. The boys rarely wanted him around because he was just a pesky little kid.

Those years Papa was sick she'd almost forget about him, but she usually knew where to find him—either sitting down by the river, fishing, or hiking across the pasture with the pole over his shoulder—bait can at the end. Poor lonely little boy.

If only Papa hadn't got sick. Hank was only nine when Papa died. He probably couldn't remember Papa taking him anywhere or doing anything with him. If only . . .

By noon Emma's head was splitting. She tried to take a nap while Jeanie was asleep, but the "if onlys" kept coming. There was no one to talk to about it. Couldn't talk about it on the phone, and, anyway, she wasn't about to confide in Ella. Ella's Carl, who was a year younger than Hank, was as ambitious as Hank was lazy.

She went to bed early that night, still bogged down in a welter of emotions and too weary to pray more than, "Father, straighten out my thinking, please. And help Henny—Hank."

Saturday, as she cleaned house, she decided digging up the past was futile. She had better think about what to do now.

Maybe if she talked to Hank—reasoned with him—helped him see what he was doing to himself.

No. She had tried that more times than she would count.

"All you do is nag me," he'd say.

If she quoted Scripture, she was preaching.

If she pointed out an error, he quickly reminded her of a time Carl or Roy had done the same thing—or something worse.

If she tried to show him she was for him, he twisted her words to sound like she was against him.

No. She couldn't reason with him. She'd learned that long ago. What could she do?

That question hung heavy over her all through church on Sunday.

When Reverend Fischer shook hands with her, he looked deep into her eyes. "Are you all right, Mrs. Verleger?"

She nodded and tried to smile.

After dinner Hank said, "Pack enough grub to last me till Wednesday. I'm gonna get down to the shack before the snow starts."

He didn't even say good-bye—just whistled for Sport and away he trudged.

She watched his blurred figure disappear over the hill.

"We're going to Phillips this afternoon," Helen said Monday morning. "Do you want to go and visit with

Nora?"

Usually Emma would have been delighted.

"Not today," she said. "I think I'll stay home."

Jeanie had just gone to sleep when Colonel barked to announce a car. It was Rev. Fischer.

"I think something is bothering you," he said, when Emma had poured him a cup of coffee. "Do you want to talk about it?"

She heaved a long sigh. "It won't be easy—but I'll try."

Rev. Fischer listened as Emma told about Hank—his self-centeredness, and how unloving he was—how unreasonable. She felt she had failed him and was afraid that Papa's illness and other situations had scarred his life.

"I must sound like a silly old fool," she said, sniffing and drying her tears.

Rev. Fischer fastened his brown eyes on hers and said, "No, you don't. You sound like a mother who cares. There's nothing wrong with that! But let's take things piece by piece.

"First of all, you're concerned about the past. You believe Romans 8:28, don't you? That all things work together for good to those who love God?"

Emma nodded. "Yes, but Hank doesn't seem to care about God. That verse wouldn't apply to him, would it?"

"Then that's the next piece we have to deal with. He needs to love God. But first he has to know that God loves him. Do you think he feels that God loves him?"

"I don't know. He blames God for the bad things that happen."

"Do you think that Hank senses that people don't love him—don't approve of him?"

"I suppose so. But he acts like he doesn't care."

"Maybe he doesn't like himself—and he can't see how anyone else, much less God, could like him."

That was a new thought. "Could that be possible?" Emma asked. "That he doesn't like himself?"

"Do you sometimes wonder if you love him?" Rev. Fischer asked.

She looked down quickly, and her face flushed.

He put his hand over hers and said quietly, "Don't feel bad that you feel that way. I know you love him. You know why?"

She shook her head.

"Because you care about him—what happens to him. Love isn't just a pleasant feeling. It's wanting the best for someone even when they aren't fun to be with at all!"

Emma blinked back tears. "Sometimes I have such awful thoughts—like wishing I had never had him."

"But you don't dwell on those thoughts, do you?"

"Oh, goodness, no!"

"Then don't feel guilty. We aren't responsible for the thoughts that pop into our minds, you know, only the ones we allow to stay there."

"But how can I help Hen—Hank?"

"Well, first of all you have to stop feeling like every wrong thing he does is because of some mistake you made. It's true that parents have great influence on their children, but the children make the final choices.

"Hank has a will of his own. You can't defend him and shield him when he makes wrong choices, but remember—our Lord can take all these things and turn them to good in his life when Hank turns to Him and lives for Him."

"But when is he going to turn to the Lord?"

"First he has to know that God loves him—and he'll get to know that when others—you—love him the way God does—just the way he is."

"But then won't Hank think I'm approving of his actions?"

"No. He knows very well what he is doing wrong.

Ask the Lord to show you the Hank he created. All the actions that grieve you are like a layer of dirt—they aren't part of the real Hank. Ask God to help you see Hank as he could be—with the sin peeled off!"

Emma laughed. "I like that."

"That's the way God loves us, because He can see us apart from our sin. We see the person and his sin together and hate the whole bundle. We need God's kind of love, don't we?"

"Oh, I should say we do. I do!"

The clock struck two, and Rev. Fischer stood to leave. Before he went he prayed with Emma.

"Remember," he said, "when you pray for Hank, it's like you hold open the door to his heart so God can do His work in it."

"Thank you so much." Emma shook her head. "You're so young. Where did you learn all these things?"

"Right here," he said, patting his pocket with his little Bible in it. "And by spending hour after hour with Him."

When he was gone, Emma sat quietly at the table. "Father," she whispered, "You are so good! You didn't let me go to Phillips and miss this precious time. You kept Jeanie asleep. Now please help me remember all Rev. Fischer said. Help me to be loving and even-tempered, even when I don't even like Hank."

Fourteen

Losses and Gains

It wasn't unusual for Nels and Minnie to bring their children over on a Sunday afternoon, so Emma wasn't surprised to look up and see their car pulling into the driveway. But immediately she sensed this visit was different. Minnie, who usually talked non-stop, was oddly quiet.

When the children ran off to play and the men were talking in a corner, Minnie sat down near Emma. "Ma, I have something to tell you. We're moving to California."

"You're *what?* "

Minnie nodded, close to tears. "Nels has been reading about it, and he thinks he can get work. It does sound wonderful, Ma."

"But when? And how will you get there?"

Then Minnie did talk non-stop, as she told how they planned to have an auction and sell everything they couldn't take with them. They would buy a tent and a camp stove, and Nels would build storage space in their model T. Her eyes sparkled.

"Oh Ma, it will be fun! Amy is ten. She's a lot of help. And Johnny is four—he isn't a baby."

"I know, but the desert—the heat—and not even a closed car."

"That's why we plan to leave in May—just as soon as school is out."

Emma tried to smile. "I've got to get used to the idea, I guess. But when will we ever see you. . . ." She put her head down to hide her tears.

"I can't think about that. You know Nels. When he makes up his mind. . . ."

Emma had tried to be cheerful, but later, in bed, she felt tears slide down her cheeks and into her pillow.

"Lord, I just get over crying about one thing, and there's another. I can't bear to think of not seeing them for years. And you know how Minnie calls me about every little thing. What will she do?"

Then she remembered what Rev. Fischer had said about God loving Hank more than she would ever love him. That's the way He loved Minnie, too.

"Lord, I'm sorry. I know you'll take care of her. Give her friends and keep them safe."

But through the next weeks Emma's heart was heavy.

It grew even heavier the first Sunday in April, when Rev. Fischer announced that he was leaving.

"First Minnie, now him," Emma said as she set the table. "I knew we wouldn't have him long. The good ones never stay long."

Minnie sent a picture post card every now and then as they headed west, but Emma yearned for the day she got one with an address on it. Three weeks on the road, and they still weren't at their destination.

"Think I have a bad case of spring fever," Emma told Helen one May morning. "I don't want to stay inside. Want to come out and see where the perennials are?"

Helen dried her hands, slipped on a sweater, and followed Emma. They made a tour of the yard and decided that Helen would have the east side of the house and front yard, Emma the west—and the "stone jar," as the planter made of field stone and mortar was called, where she always planted her red carnations.

Emma raked leaves away from the sprouting iris, bleeding heart, peonies, and tiger lilies while Jeanie romped with Colonel. Tomorrow she'd work on the west side of the house—plant a little honeysuckle and dig a new flower bed.

"When the roll—is called up yon-der," she sang, thinking surely there couldn't be anyone more content and happy than she. Could it be possible that a year ago she had been so upset abut Roy getting married?. Now that her life had settled down, she was glad she didn't have the care of the whole house. It was enough to take care of her two rooms and Carl and Hank's bedrooms.

One of these years, when Carl got married, she'd fix his room for Jeanie. There was a heat vent in the ceiling above her stove that went up into that room. But she wouldn't think about that for a long time.

It was June before Minnie wrote and sent them her address. Emma promptly wrote and told her bits of news, including the arrival of George and Sadie's new little daughter, Betty.

Several weeks later Hank said he'd be going with Carl out to Devil's Lake, North Dakota, to work in the harvest fields.

"That should be good for him," she told Roy. "He needs to get out in the world a little. Maybe he'll think of something beside trapping and the woods."

With only Jeanie and herself to wash and cook for, Emma had time to go visiting a little more. She loved to go over and help Ella and hold little Jimmy.

He was a cute little fellow but, she told Helen, "I'm afraid he is going to be one spoiled child. The older children cater to him something awful."

By July the paper was full of Al Smith and Herbert Hoover.

"Who are you going to vote for, Ma?" Ella asked one day as Emma shelled peas.

"Well, it won't be Al Smith. I was reading that he's against prohibition."

"But things haven't gone too well, with all the bootlegging and bathtub gin and everything. People are getting poisoned—"

"Humph!" Emma interrupted. "Serves 'em right for drinking the stuff. Like I always say—"

"Oh Ma, don't start! I know you hate drinking. But do you really think Hoover can put a chicken in every pot and a car in every garage like he's promising?"

Emma laughed. "Don't know as I've ever seen a politician's promises kept—but who knows? Time someone got in there and did something for farmers for once, instead of only bankers and businessmen."

In September, Carl and Hank came back from out west. Carl stayed long enough for Emma to do his laundry, and then took off for Muskegon. Didn't seem like he was going to be home much anymore. He wrote that he had a job at Continental Motors and then, a few weeks later, that he had been laid off and was in Hart doing odd jobs for room and board.

In November, Emma was among the happy ones when Herbert Hoover was elected president.

"Now we'll see who'll have chickens in the pot," she said to Ella.

Day after day that month, Emma waited for another letter from Carl. The next time she wrote she enclosed a stamped envelope.

That brought an answer. Carl wanted to come home, but he didn't have the twenty dollars it would cost. Would she send it?

The money was in the mail the next day.

The evening Carl came home, Emma let Jeanie up past her bedtime and sit on Carl's lap while he told about his experiences.

"When I went to put in my application at Continental Motors, they said I had to go to a high school principal and get a work permit, because I wasn't twenty-one. They gave me a form to fill out and, along with a lot of other stuff, they wanted the names and ages of my brothers and sisters.

"Well, I started with Al; I knew he was 41. I sure didn't know all the other ages, so I just put each one down two years younger than the last one. But when I had about seven of 'em down, I heard the secretary snicker, and I could feel my ears gettin' red. I kept writin', but before I got to Roy I had all the spaces filled up, and that woman laughed right out loud.

"The principal came and looked and said, 'Quite a family you have there.' But he was real nice and gave me my permit. I got out of there fast!"

Emma and Carl and Hank were laughing, so Jeanie laughed right with them. She laughed and laughed, and the grown-ups laughed with her until none of them could remember why they had been laughing in the first place.

It was good to have Carl home.

Fifteen

Trip to Muskegon

A trip! A real, honest-to-goodness, stay overnight on the way trip! It sounded wonderful that April day, when Gertie asked Emma to come along with them to visit Fred and Helen in Muskegon.

"But it will cost so much money!" Emma protested, predictably.

"Ma, we're going anyway. It won't cost any more for you and Jeanie to ride along."

"But we'll have to stay overnight and eat in restaurants and everything."

Gertie pumped a pan of water from her cistern pump before she sat down at the table with Emma, eyes shining. "Oh, it will be fun! We'll go around the lake on the way there, and coming back we'll cross on the ferry. And Fred says just wait'll we see their beach—snow white sand! Won't the kids have fun?"

"That's another thing—the three of them riding all that way."

Gertie dismissed that problem with a wave of her hand. "Did you ever see two kids play better together than Earl and Jeanie—and Clyde is so quiet—thank goodness! Oh, I wish it was June now, instead of April!"

Emma never did actually say she'd go—it was simply taken for granted that she would. She ordered some dress material, pulled the sewing machine into her room, and sewed a dress for Jeanie and one for herself.

"Does Jeanie have a bathing suit?" Helen asked one day in May.

"Oh, for goodnes sakes, I never thought of that. No, she doesn't."

"I've got an idea." Helen went upstairs and came back with a long red and blue stocking cap—the kind that hangs way down the back. "We could make her one from this. Cut the neck and arm holes and legs, and crochet around them."

"Why, I'd never have thought of that! Of course! I'd hate to have to buy one."

While Emma sewed dresses, Helen worked on the bathing suit.

One day Gertie called and said, "Joe says you should stay overnight here the night before we leave. We'll get the kids up and leave at five."

"I feel like a little kid counting days," Emma told Helen. "I've packed that suitcase mentally half a dozen times already."

The afternoon before they were to leave, Roy took them to Gertie's and carried in Emma's straw suitcase—the one Papa had bought when he was on the town board and had to stay overnight in Phillips.

"Have a good trip, Ma," Roy said. "We'll take good care of your chickens. You greet Fred and Helen for me."

That evening Jeanie perched on Gertie's kitchen stool while Joe cut her hair straight around even with the bottom of her ears.

"Who are we going to see on our trip?" Gertie asked her, smoothing her shiny bangs.

"Uncle Fred and Aunt Helen and Kermit and Everett!" she answered, waving her arms and kicking her feet as she talked.

"And that's supposed to sit still for two days in the car?" Emma said behind her hand.

As they rode along, Clyde kept Jeanie singing. When the children would grow too restless, Joe would stop and let them stretch.

That evening they stopped in a tourist home. Emma woke the next morning to the lonesome whistle of a train. Where was she?

She opened her eyes and saw pink rosebud wallpaper and soft light flowing in around the edges of the window shade. The tourist room!

Joy flooded in. Today she'd see Fred, Helen, and the little boys! She wanted to jump right up and get going, but there wasn't a sound in the house, and Jeanie lay asleep beside her.

"Oh, Father. You're so good! Thank you for this trip. Thank you for this soft bed and the good sleep. Lord, help me be patient and loving—all that you want me to be today. And keep us safe as we travel."

Jeanie stirred, opened her eyes and said, "Mama? Where are we?"

"We're in a tourist room, remember?" Emma whispered.

Jeanie yawned and sat up. "What's a tourist?"

"Someone who travels. We are tourists."

"Are we always gonna be tourists?"

Emma chuckled. "No. Only while we're on our trip. Say! Do you know what's going to happen today?"

Jeanie sprang up and started bouncing on the bed. "We're gonna get to Uncle Fred's house!"

"Shh! And don't jump on the bed! Let's get dressed. I hear Earl and Clyde." Emma and Jeanie were ready when Gertie knocked on the door.

As they stood outside waiting for Joe to tie the luggage on the top of the car, Emma looked up at the big white house they had slept in. "Don't you wonder why people with such a fine house like this take in tourists?"

"Didn't you see the man sitting in the wheelchair way back in the house when we came in last night?" Gertie asked.

"No, I didn't. I was watching Jeanie so she wouldn't touch anything." A cloud of sadness drifted over Emma's joy as they drove away. "Lord, bless them," she whispered.

Fred had just got home from work when they pulled up in front of the little gray-shingled house with a rose trellis in front.

"Ma! You don't look a day older!" Fred exclaimed as he hugged her. "A bit grayer, though."

"And fatter! Never been this heavy in my life! You look good, Fred."

While the grown-ups exchanged greetings, the four boys eyed each other and then ran off to see the rabbits—Jeanie right behind them.

"She looks so much like Emmie," Fred said.

"Doesn't act like her, though," Emma said. "She talks, talks, talks—just like her dad."

Fred laughed. "As I remember, Emmie always had plenty to say."

"I suppose—but Jeanie's different."

After supper, as they sat around the table, Emma said, "Isn't it wonderful how the years melt away once we're together again? Doesn't seem it could be five years since we've seen each other."

The next day they went to the beach, and Emma could hardly believe her eyes. The sand was white. The children played at the edge of the water while the grown-ups visited in the shade.

"I see I don't have to be concerned about Jeanie when Kermit's around, " Emma said. "Look at him!"

"He adores her," Helen said. "He asked me last night if he could use some money from his piggy bank to buy something for her."

Sunday Joe stayed home with the children so the others could go to church. When they returned, Jeanie ran out of the house wailing, "Mama! Mama!" She hung onto Emma's skirt for dear life.

Emma took her in her arms and sat down on the steps. "*Liebchen!* What's the matter?"

Joe came out, shaking his head. "She lay on the bed and cried all the while you were gone! Couldn't do a thing with her."

"She's with me all the time," Emma said lamely. "I don't know what we'll do when it's time for her to start school."

That afternoon Fred sat down near Emma on the front porch. "Haven't had a chance to talk to you. How are things going with you and Roy's wife?"

"We get along real well. Oh, we do things differently, but we put up with each other."

"And her?" Fred nodded toward Jeanie.

"The hardest part is always wondering if I'm doing the right thing. I feel a different kind of responsibility than I did with you kids."

Jeanie came to have Emma unbuckle her shoe, so she could get the sand out.

"It makes such a difference, being older," Emma said with a sigh. "If only I can live till she's through school." She dumped the sand over the railing and put Jeanie's shoe back on her. "There now. Better stay on the sidewalk."

Quickly Fred changed the subject. "Al wrote that business has been bad at the blacksmith shop. He's thinking about coming to work here."

The morning of their departure, Gertie stood on the ferry deck and took a deep breath. "This is how the ocean must be. Can't see a bit of land."

A gust of wind picked Joe's flat straw hat off his head, and they watched it fly away.

"I want to look and look so hard that I'll never forget all this blue," Emma said. "Just think, Gert, when we get home and we're ironing or washing dishes, we'll still see this in our mind's eye."

Gertie laughed. "Aren't you glad you came?"

They couldn't find tourist rooms in a private home that night, so they went to a hotel. Emma had never seen so much glass and silver as in that dining room. She spread the huge white napkin on Jeanie's lap and prayed she wouldn't spill her milk.

What luxury! A bathroom with each room! Jeanie reveled in the big white tub until Emma said, "Look at your feet! They're wrinkled as a prune." She lifted her out, protesting, and wrapped her in a fluffy white towel.

The closer they got to home, the more eager Emma became. She had never been away from home this long since Hank was a baby, eighteen years ago. She and Al had gone to Oshkosh and to Wind Lake to see their birthplaces, but she got so homesick they came home sooner than they had planned.

"I just don't know how to thank you," she told Joe when he carried in her suitcase.

Jeanie grabbed his hand. "Bye, Daddy Joe," she said softly.

He gave her a hug and went off chuckling.

"It was good to go, but it's good to be home again," Emma told Roy and Helen.

In mid-August Len called to say that Nora had given birth to a boy.

"What did you name him?"

"Leonard Junior, of course. What else?"

Emma told Ella about her visit to see the baby a couple weeks later.

"Dimple in the chin just like his dad. Think he might have the Verleger ears, too. But, oh, I was so embarrassed! Jeanie ran in with Joy Ann, and by the time I got in there she was washing the bathroom! Her straw hat was still hanging down her back, and there she was—washing the sink, walls, floor, everything—with a nice, white washcloth. And you know what a good house-keeper Nora is!"

Ella laughed. "What did Nora say?"

"Oh, she laughed and laughed. We stood and watched for a few minutes—she wouldn't let me get after her. Said she'd remind her in about twenty years and see if she still liked cleaning bathrooms that well!"

On Sunday when Gertie came for a little visit, she said, "Guess what? I'm going to board the school teacher. She seems like a friendly young lady. Her name's Olga Harrold—tiny little girl."

"That will be nice for you," Emma replied. "Joe is gone so much, it'll be nice to have someone to talk with. I remember how I enjoyed having Jenny Clark with us when Papa was working in the woods. I'd knit or mend, and she'd read to me."

Gertie laughed. "Well, I don't know if Miss Harrold will read to me, but I'm looking forward to having her with us."

In September Ed and Connie wrote that they had another little boy, Richard. He promised that *next* summer they would be sure to get home.

It was evident that Helen and Roy were going to be parents, too, sometime in the winter. Usually women talked about their expected babies, but Helen didn't say a word, and Emma didn't ask.

When Hank got home from the harvest fields that fall, he was more talkative and enthusiastic than Emma had seen him in years.

"I'm gonna get a radio," he announced one day. "Gotta set a couple poles for an aerial—that's to catch the sound waves," he explained.

"What next," Emma muttered as she watched the boys struggle to set the thirty-foot poles.

They strung wire between them and brought it through little insulators on the porch and through a hole in the north window.

Emma hoped it would sound better than Gertie's radio. All she had ever heard on it was a lot of crackling they called static.

"I'm gonna need this table," Hank said, taking the pictures and magazines off the walnut table.

Emma didn't protest. It was good to see him interested in something new.

"You'll like it, Ma, " he said. "You can hear music anytime you want to without even changing records."

Hark suddenly acquired several friends who came and listened to the radio with him until all hours of the night.

"I'm actually getting so I can sleep with all that racket," she told Ella. "At least I know he's home and safe."

Emma shouldn't have been surprised when Al and Mamie came and told her he was closing up the blacksmith shop and leaving for Muskegon before school started. Mamie and the children would stay with Mamie's folks until he got settled.

"I guess it wouldn't seem so far away if we hadn't just driven there," Emma told Gertie.

She was determined not to make leaving any harder for Al, but it wasn't easy. She had gone to her "patterns" seeking the right attitude. The Bible didn't say if that virtuous woman in Proverbs ever had to cope with her family members moving away, but the I Corinthians verses gave her direction.

Emma saw that the loving thing to do was not to concentrate on her own sense of loss, but to be patient, kind, and to hope. She would not think, "I won't see them for years," but, "They will come to visit or I'll go there."

It wasn't so easy to bring her feelings into line. The day after Al and Mamie's auction, as scenes of the torn-up household set her heart aching, she talked it out with the Lord.

"You're going to have to help me, Lord. I'm counting on you to give me your peace, so I can think about them and not myself."

The end of October brought two newsworthy events: another baby--George, Jr.--for George and Sadie, and the stock market crash.

"This crash business is all that's in the papers these days," Emma complained to Helen. "I don't understand what it's all about."

Helen said she didn't know a lot about it, either. Evidently many people thought life wasn't worth living when they lost their money, she reported, because that day's paper said many were jumping out of windows.

"Oh, my goodness! Guess we can't understand what it would be like to lose everything."

"But money isn't everything," Helen protested.

Emma agreed. "It certainly isn't—but a lot of people haven't found that out."

Sixteen

Visits from the Doctor

Christmas night Jeanie woke up crying and feverish. For the next three days neither she nor Emma slept for more than an hour at a time as the fever raged on. The fourth morning her forehead and chest were covered with a rash—measles.

"How did I ever take care of all those sick children through the years?" Emma asked herself. She was exhausted caring for one little measly girl.

By January fourth the rash had faded and the fever was down, but Emma still tried to keep Jeanie quiet and warm.

When she went to the separator room to get milk that morning, Helen wasn't around.

Roy came downstairs smiling. "This is it! I've called Doc, and Leonard is bringing Helen's mother over."

"How's she doing?"

Roy shrugged. "Good. She says she doesn't have pain—just knows something's going on."

"I've heard of women like that," Emma said with a rueful laugh, "but I never knew any."

Emma kept the door closed so Jeanie wouldn't be aware anything unusual was happening, but when Mrs. Risberg and the doctor came, she got excited.

It was late afternoon when Roy came downstairs saying, "It's a boy! We've named him Ronald Risberg."

A baby! Right in the house! Jeanie hopped up and squealed, begging to see him right away.

The doctor said the baby had a natural immunity to measles, so Mrs. Risberg brought the baby for them to see—but Emma kept Jeanie a good distance from him anyway.

"He'll be here all the time. You'll be able to see him every day."

"Ma," Roy said, coughing as he talked, "if you want to call the girls, go ahead. I don't feel so good."

She felt his brow. "My land, boy! You're burning up! Have you had the measles?"

"Not that I remember."

"Good thing you have that hired man. Let him do the chores tonight. You stay in."

That night Emma had Lloyd bring down a mattress for Roy to sleep on. He didn't get up for chores the next morning, and three days later he broke out with measles.

Mrs. Risberg took full charge of Helen and the baby, and Emma kept the heater roaring and did what she could for Roy, trying meanwhile to keep Jeanie quiet.

Dr. McKinnon had insisted that Helen stay in bed ten days. Four more days and she could sit up. Emma made brief visits upstairs, but was still afraid she'd carry germs.

That weekend Carl and Hank came home from camp, and Carl offered to stay home.

"Naw, I'll be up in a couple days," Roy said. "Lloyd can handle the chores till then."

But by Tuesday Roy had chills and fever.

"This isn't right," Emma said, tucking the comforter around his shaking shoulders. "You were starting to feel better, and the rash is gone. We'd better have the doctor check you."

Roy was too sick to protest.

Down on his knees beside Roy, Dr. McKinnon thumped and listened. He stood up, frowning, and said to Emma, "Pneumonia. Right lung's really bad. Keep him warm, give him lots of liquids, and I'll leave some medicine to help him cough up that stuff."

Pneumonia. The dreaded word echoed in Emma's ears. There was nothing doctors could do but hope the patient's body was strong enough to fight it. Emmie's hadn't been. First the child-bed fever infection, then pneumonia.

But Roy was strong. He had been healthy, up to the time he got measles.

Her hand shook as she poured coffee for the doctor.

Mrs. Risberg read fear in her eyes when Emma told her what the doctor had said. "He'll be all right," she said assuringly, "but Helen had better stay upstairs another day or two."

"There's got to be more I can do," Emma told herself. First of all, she could pray, and pray she did—fervently, tearfully, as she fed the chickens and washed the dishes and looked after Jeanie.

So cold! Must fight cold air. Keep Roy protected. Each time someone opened the kitchen door, frigid air swept through the house. Emma cringed, imagining it attacking Roy through every thin spot in the covers and blowing icy shafts down around his neck.

She lined chairs along the foot of his mattress and draped blankets over them. Whenever she walked past she hunted for gaps she might have missed and pinned them shut.

At noon she had Lloyd bring in a bucket of oats. She filled ten-pound sugar sacks and heated them in the oven. These she tucked along Roy's back and chest as he rested on his side. Every hour or so she'd replace them with warm ones.

One time she'd find him chilled; the next drenched

with perspiration. She'd help him strip off a soggy flannel night shirt and don a dry one. She tore pieces of soft rags for him to use for handkerchieves and set a bag beside him to put them in. When it was full, she burned it.

The washtub didn't get put away those days. It stood in the corner of Helen's kitchen when Mrs. Risberg wasn't washing for Helen and the baby, or Emma doing the rest of the laundry. The drying rack behind the stove was never empty.

During the day, distractions kept fear at the fringes of her thoughts. Emma usually slept soundly from sheer exhaustion for the first part of the night. Every hour, though, she'd wake up, as though she had a built-in alarm clock. She would fix the fires, change the grain bags, and do what she could for Roy. Immediately, she'd go back to sleep for another hour—until four o'clock or so.

Then, brain alert, body still exhausted, she'd wage the thought-battle. She was a doe chased to the point of collapse by a pack of wolves, surrounded by fear-thoughts intent on destroying her.

Pneumonia. You know he's getting worse. His lungs are filling, filling. You thought Papa couldn't die. But he did. You thought Emmie couldn't die. But she did. You think Roy can't die. But—NO! Lord, help me!

And she'd come awake with a start, safe in bed. *The fires. The grain bags.*

Back in bed she'd whisper, " 'Thou wilt keep him in perfect peace, whose mind is stayed on thee; because he trusteth in thee.' Father, I trust you. You promised that all things work together for good to them that love you. You know I love you." And another hour of sleep was hers.

From night to night the fear-thoughts and subsequent words of comfort varied, but not the pattern—until several nights after the doctor had been there. Toward morning the thoughts began to plague her again, and she felt anger boil up within her.

"In the name of Jesus," she spat out, "leave me alone!" The thoughts fled, and she slept.

Thursday morning Helen came down, smiling but pale—her mother and the baby right behind her. Roy propped himself up on his elbow to see the baby and immediately began to cough.

Emma didn't blame Helen for wanting to come downstairs, but she was concerned about having them close to Roy.

Helen wasn't afraid. She had Lloyd bring a narrow cot down from upstairs, and that's where she nursed the baby and slept at night. The baby slept in a clothes basket she had painted ivory.

Roy still had terrible spells of coughing and alternately burned and perspired, but he seemed more alert. Small wonder, with Helen and the baby right there to motivate him.

The day after Helen came downstairs, her brother, Leonard, came and got his mother.

"They'll be fine," Emma assured Mrs. Risberg, but she was weary. The washing, cooking, fire-tending, nursing she could handle. It was trying to keep Jeanie quiet that exasperated her. The child needed to run and jump—but where? How?

She looked out of the window and saw Lloyd piling wood. That noon she asked him if he'd mind if Jeanie came out to "help."

Lloyd said he certainly could use some help, so out went Jeanie in her brown coat and leggings to help him pile wood.

"Bless that boy," Emma whispered as she shut the door behind them.

Now to work without tripping over Jeanie and without answering one single question! Or should she take a nap? How long, she wondered, would her body stay well with these jack-in-the-box nights? What would happen to the family if she got sick?

"I'm going to take a little nap while Jeanie's out," she told Roy and Helen.

Oh, that bed felt good!

"Jesus," she whispered, "You said all that were weary and heavy laden should come to you for rest. I come to you now. Restore me. Keep me strong."

When she heard Jeanie on the porch she got up, smoothed her hair, slipped on her glasses, and set her face smiling.

The next day Lloyd took Jeanie to the barn to help him feed the cattle at noon.

"Father, you are answering my prayer for help and I thank you," she whispered, and off she went to bed.

When Lloyd came in for supper Friday evening, he was coughing the same dry cough Roy had started with.

"Oh, no! " Emma groaned. "Let me feel your forehead."

"I'm all right," he insisted.

"No, you aren't! You have a fever. Have you had measles?"

He shrugged. "I don't know."

Emma shook her finger at him. "You're going right up to bed. We can't have you down with pneumonia, too."

"But the milking?"

"I can do it. There aren't that many cows milking now."

She heard Roy groan.

"Can't we call some neighbor to help?" Helen suggested.

They tried to think of someone they might call, but most of the men were working in camp, and women and children were doing chores.

"I can manage," Emma insisted, as she tied on her *Kopftuch*.

Colonel barked, announcing a car.

Emma opened the door. "Carl! Are we glad to see you!"

Carl launched into a whole string of reasons why he had quit his job, but Emma didn't hear. She was busy thanking the Lord.

Helen began cooking again and took care of Roy, so Emma stayed in her own rooms more. Sunday Roy sat up in the rocker a little while. Emma hardly dared believe he was better. But when he started putting wood in the stove on Monday, she knew it was true.

"Praise God, Praise God," she whispered as she worked.

Emma felt sorry for Lloyd, alone upstairs, and tried to go up to see him often during the day. She knew Roy hated to tell him that he wouldn't need him any longer, now that Carl was home, but Lloyd had anticipated it. He asked Carl to take him home as soon as he was feeling better.

Life became more routine once more. The highlight of Jeanie's day was baby Ronnie's bath. Of course she wanted to bathe her dolls, but Emma explained that the cloth dolls couldn't be put in water. Emma made tiny flannel diapers so Jeanie could change her dolls, and one day Helen powdered them. She was delighted because they smelled "just like baby Ronnie—when he didn't need to be changed."

One day in February Emma watched Roy stride across the yard with an arm full of wood. Gratitude welled up inside her again, and wondered if God were tired of hearing her thank him.

Hank came home from camp and helped Roy with chores, and Carl took a job driving a truck. He stayed at a tiny hotel in Ogema.

"We've been seeing a lot of Carl lately," Gertie told Emma a few weeks later. "He comes over several nights a week."

"That's nice," Emma said. "He gets lonesome for the family."

Gertie laughed. "Well, Ma, I don't think that's quite the reason. Looks to me like Cupid's at work."

"You mean Carl and Miss Harrold . . .?"

"It's a little soon to tell, but I'm hoping it's serious. You know what a special little gal she is."

Emma decided not to tell anyone yet, but she was delighted. Where on earth would they live, though? Carl didn't have any savings or even a steady job. And Gertie said Olga helped her mother a lot, because she was rearing several children alone.

Oh, well, they'll find a way. Young lovers have a way of doing that.

In April Gertie called with the latest news. "Last night Joe had to meet the train at Spencer, and he asked Carl to drive him over. I had a notion that Carl wanted to ask Olga to go along, so I ducked into the pantry. I could see them through the crack in the door. She was sitting by the table doing some school work, and Carl stood there shuffling his feet and jingling the change in his pocket. Finally he said, 'Ah, I'm taking Joe to catch the train at Spencer, an' I was wondering—you wanna go along for the exercise?' "

Emma laughed. When she'd caught her breath, she said, "Well, did she?"

"Don't know if she went along for the exercise, but she went!"

"Oh, I can just see him."

"I think she really likes him, Ma. When he told her he's going to work for Len next week, she looked real disappointed. Won't see him night after night, like she does now."

In May, Ed wrote that they were coming home in June. "Can't wait to see them," Emma told Ella.

"Imagine little Connie with five children. Wonder if she'll look a lot older."

"I can't imagine Ed with five children," Ella said. "But I bet he's a good father."

When Minnie's letter came soon after, Emma didn't know who to call first. She finally settled on Gertie.

"Nels and Minnie are coming back from California! Nels has a mechanic job at Kiger's garage in Ogema!"

They got back the second week in June and rented a house about a mile east of Ogema.

Ed and Connie came the last week in June. Ed hugged Emma so tight it hurt. "Oh Ma, it's good to see you!"

"Connie! You still look like a little school girl!" Emma exclaimed.

Connie laughed. "I can tell you, I don't feel like one!"

What a commotion! Jeanie stood and watched at first, but in a little while she was running and chasing with Ed and Connie's five children.

"Such a little cutie, Grandma," Connie said as she watched her. "Looks like the little girl in the Jell-o advertisement."

Every day they visited one of the families. Sometimes Emma and Jeanie went along, but some days Emma stayed home to catch up a bit. Jeanie wouldn't go without her.

"I'm worried," Emma told Connie. "She starts school this fall and she doesn't want to go anywhere without me."

"Oh, she'll be all right when she sees the other kids. She enjoys being with them so much."

Emma sighed. " I hope so."

Each evening, when they came home from visiting somewhere, Connie would nurse the baby while Ed would washed up the other children and helped them get ready for bed—laughing, singing, and teasing all the while.

"Does my heart good to see them," Emma said to herself. "The way they look at each other. . . and they enjoy those little ones so much. Such a happy little family."

Seventeen

Still Learning to Trust

In August Helen had a phone call. "That was Ruth Anderson, the new school teacher," she reported. "She needs a place to board and wondered if we'd be interested."

"Hmm. Ruth's a quiet, pleasant young lady. She'd be nice to have around—and the money would come in handy. But I hate to give up Hank's or Carl's room."

"How about the one at the top of the stairs?"

"It doesn't have a heat vent in it."

"We could leave the stair door open, and she could leave her door ajar."

Ruth came over and said the room would be fine. Helen and Emma papered it with blue flowered paper, and Helen added new woven rugs and white ruffled curtains. Ruth would be surprised when she saw it again.

Before school started, Emma went along to Tomahawk and bought a little red pencil box and a lunch box with Red Riding Hood on it. Then she bought a can of salmon and a loaf of bakery rye bread for Jeanie's school lunches.

The first day of school Jeanie ate little breakfast—

and what she ate came right back up. Emma wasn't surprised. The first day of school was bound to be hard for her.

Roy drove them the half mile because it was raining, and Emma took her in. She was about to cry, when the older girls rushed over and gathered her in. Emma quickly left.

That night Jeanie talked and talked, and Emma sighed a deep sigh. She liked it!

But the following morning, up came the breakfast again.

Emma walked Jeanie to the fence line, but when she turned to go home, Jeanie ran back and clung to her. Arvid Johnson saved the day when he stopped and asked if she'd like a ride. Reluctantly, she climbed in beside Donald, who was a year older.

The next morning she threw up again. Emma walked her way to the top of the hill, until she could see the school, and Jeanie went the rest of the way alone . . . crying.

"I don't know what to do," Emma told Ella. "I feel sorry for her, but she has to go to school."

"Does she say why she doesn't want to go?"

"No. She just cries when I ask her. And no matter what she eats, it ends up in the slop pail."

Emma talked to Miss Anderson, who said Jeanie was fine once she got there. She seemed to be a bright little girl.

All through September, October, and November, Jeanie begged to stay home. Every morning her stomach was upset. Emma packed extra lunch for her, and she did eat something at morning recess and would keep it down.

One snowy day, Ella called and said Henry was taking the children to school on the logging sleigh, and they'd come around and pick up Jeanie. But by the time they came, Jeanie had decided she wasn't going. Emma dressed her in spite of her balking and walked out with her, but she wouldn't get on the sleigh. Henry got down, picked her up, and put her on, but she jumped off and ran to the house.

Emma waved them on then, and helped Jeanie take off her coat and overshoes. "Jeanie, you must go to school," she told her, but Jeanie just continued to cry. Emma sat down in her rocker and cried, too.

After a few minutes she dried her tears, went to the bedroom, and pulled her straw suitcase out from under the bed. "Well, Jeanie," she said, "if you won't go to school here, I'll have to send you to your dad."

"No, Mama! No, Mama!" she screamed. "I'll go!"

Emma held her close, and they both cried; then Emma put the suitcase back under the bed.

The next morning Jeanie lost her breakfast, but she went to school without a fuss.

The excitement of the up-coming Christmas program kept her going, and Emma hoped she'd be better when school started up again after Christmas. If she wasn't, Emma would have to take her to the doctor.

Miss Anderson still didn't understand it. "She enjoys school and she gets along well with the other children."

Dr. McKinnon poked and prodded and pointed his little light in Jeanie's eyes, ears, and mouth saying, "Hmm. Hmm."

When he finished he said, "Nothing wrong except she has a nervous stomach. She'll outgrow it. Give her cod liver oil every evening to build her up a little."

Emma thanked him as she helped Jeanie with her coat. "I'm glad there's nothing seriously wrong. It's so different from raising my own. I'm just too old, I guess. If I can just live till she's through school. . . ."

Dr. McKinnon's eyebrows shot up. "Jeanie," he said, "go wait with Uncle Roy. Grandma will be right out."

He took Emma's arm and ushered her back into his

examining room. "Sit down, Mrs. Verleger," he said, and he sat down opposite her. "Do you remember the last words you said a few minutes ago?"

"I think I said I hoped I'd live till Jeanie was through school."

"You did." He reached over and took her hand. "Now, if you were a little girl and you heard your grandma say that. . . ."

Emma's lip trembled. "Oh, my goodness. You mean she's scared?"

"It's just a guess. Maybe she doesn't actually think it out, but way down she feels that if she doesn't go to school, she won't ever get through school—and you won't die."

Emma shook her head. "I never realized. . . ."

"I know you didn't," he said gently "I don't think it will do any good to try to explain it to her—just don't ever say those words again!"

That night, after Jeanie was in bed, Emma talked it over with Roy, Helen, and Miss Anderson.

"I have an idea," Miss Anderson said. "How would it be if I asked her to walk with me in the morning—to 'help' me, before school.

The next morning Emma held her breath as Miss Anderson made her suggestion. Jeanie was delighted! Away she trotted beside Miss Anderson, feeling important. That was the last of the upset stomach.

In January Ed wrote that he and Connie were expecting another baby at the end of February. Emma stuck the letter back in the envelope with a sigh. Was this the way her mother had felt, each time she had announced that another baby was on the way? Well, she consoled herself, they certainly were getting along well, and were all healthy and happy last summer. They'd manage one more.

The first Sunday in February, Gertie, Joe and the boys

came for dinner. "How's Carl's romance coming along?" Emma asked. Joe chuckled, and Gertie shook her head.

"Joe isn't helping it any. How he teases that poor girl. Last week she waited for a letter day after day, and none came. On Friday she picked up the Rabinowich ad—you know, that store in Phillips—and there were *three* letters stuck in the ad!

"Why, Joe!" Emma said, trying not to smile. "Shame on you!"

Ed and Connie's announcement came the last week of the month. Little Eddie had been born the twenty-first.

Emma tried to imagine Roy's little Ronnie with a new brother or sister already. Though he was walking well and saying a few words, he still seemed like a baby.

A week later Ed phoned. Connie was in the hospital in Durand—childbed fever.

Emma sank into the nearest chair. "Not little Connie!"

She could see her as she was last summer—short brown hair bouncing as she walked, smooth young arms holding the baby and Mary Lou clinging to her skirt.

"Oh, Lord, no! Don't let her die!" Not once in her memory had a woman ever survived childbed fever. "There must be something the doctors can do. It can't be your will that these young mothers die!"

She called the girls, and they tried to sound hopeful, but their was fear in their voices.

That night Emma slept little and prayed much. "Father, Jesus said that whatever we asked of you in His name, believing, you'll give to us. I pray for Connie's recovery. Your word says 'with God, nothing is impossible'. I want to believe that. Help me!"

Ed wrote hopeful letters, and Emma clung to his words. But on March twenty-first, he phoned.

"Mama, can you come? I need you."

Emma took Jeanie out of school, and the next day Roy drove them to Eau Galle.

Ed tried to be cheerful—especially at the hospital in front of Connie, who lay pale and hollow-eyed on the high bed.

She smiled at Jeanie. "Hello, little Jell-o-girl. Come give Auntie a kiss."

Jeanie shrank back.

"That's all right," Connie said. "I don't look very kissable, do I?"

Each night Emma prayed, "Father, I ask you, for the sake of all the husbands and all the children who could be left, to help someone discover a medicine for childbed fever. I know you don't want these mothers to die."

During the day Jeanie played happily with her children, but at bedtime she often cried. One night she said, "I don't want Aunt Connie to die! Why can't God make her well, like He did in the Bible?"

"I don't know, *Liebchen*," Emma replied. "God doesn't do miracles anymore—at least I never heard of any."

Jeanie rolled over and put her face in her pillow, but Emma could hear her muffled words. "I don't like God!"

Emma turned her over, lifted her sullen little chin with her finger, and said, "No, *Liebchen*, don't be angry at God. God is a loving God. Maybe we just don't know what He wants us to do. He has all the instructions for how we are to live in the Bible, but maybe we just haven't found them all yet."

Jeanie reached up and hugged Emma. "I don't wanna be mad at God."

"Neither do I, *Liebchen*, neither do I."

Connie was getting worse. When Ed left for the hospital the third day, he said, "I won't be back now until she's gone. . . ."

Emma overheard the children talking.

"Poor Mama," said Little Maybelle said.

"What do you mean, 'poor Mama'?" replied Shirley. "She'll be in heaven. Poor *us!* Who's going to take care of *us*, when Daddy's on the mail route?"

The next morning Ed came home. Emma met him at the door, where they clung to each other and cried until they heard the children coming downstairs.

"Mama's gone to be with Jesus," Ed told them. The girls cried, but Allison set his little jaw and blinked hard.

By evening the first carload of brothers and sisters arrived. More came the next day.

Emma longed to find time and a place to cry, but there was too much to be done.

Connie, dressed in a lovely rose-colored dress, was laid out at her parents' home. They took the older children to see her. Again the girls cried—but not Allison.

Emma couldn't stop trembling the day of the funeral. She barely heard what the minister said. But she was relieved to see Allison cling to his daddy and cry and cry.

Out of the church—into cars—past the house—out of the cars. . . . Emma stared at the flowers piled high. Would they be able to see them from Ed's kitchen window, she wondered. Why did that cemetery have to be so close?

Some of the family went home that afternoon, but Ella, Roy, Emma, and Jeanie stayed until the next morning. When they were ready to leave, Ed picked up little Dickie and, with the four older children clustered about him, came outside to see them off. Baby Eddie was asleep in the house.

Ella and Emma struggled to keep smiling until they were out of the driveway, but they were miles away before they dried their eyes.

It was later that day that someone mentioned the date. Emma gasped. It was Jeanie's seventh birthday. They stopped and got ice cream cones to celebrate.

When they reached home they learned it was another

little girl's birthday as well—George and Sadie had a new little girl, Bunetta.

Emma felt a pang of fear, imagining George, too, standing alone with his little ones. And the April sunshine couldn't burn away the grief cloud that hung over Emma.

"If only I was closer—could help Ed," she said to Gertie one day.

"I know, Ma, you want to help all of us. But you're only one person. Sit down and have a cup of tea. I have something to tell you."

Emma sat. "What's the big news?"

Gertie leaned close, although there was no one else in the house. "This is a secret. I heard Carl and Olga talking the other day—they're planning to get married in June!"

"Oh, I'm glad! Goodness knows they don't have any money—but they'll manage somehow."

"They're just going off over a weekend by themselves."

"Ohh." Emma sounded disappointed. "I'd like to see them get married."

Gertie sighed. "I would too, but they said no matter how small and simple they made it, it would be too costly. And with this family, there's no way to keep it small."

Before Emma had had time to absorb that piece of good news, Gertie said she had more to tell. "I'm so excited! I'm going to have a baby in August."

Emma set her cup down with a clatter. "You are! Why, I never suspected."

"I've been feeling great. Just think! Maybe I'll get my little girl yet!"

Emma tried to share her enthusiasm, but she was glad to see Roy coming up the walk.

"Gertie's having a baby in August," she told him in the car.

"Good!" he said. "Bet she's hoping for a girl."

How can young people be so glib? Emma thought. *We've just seen Connie lying there. . . .*

She longed to pour out her fears to someone, but she was too ashamed. *I should have more faith,* she scolded herself. *I should be the one they can lean on—and here I am with this knot of fear inside of me.*

She grew impatient to the point of exasperation with Jeanie, was irritated with Helen, and didn't even welcome Ronnie's happy face when he came for a horsey ride on her foot. Her throat ached, her head ached, and no matter what she ate, her stomach felt queasy.

The third day—the warmest of the season, so far— Emma put on a sweater and overshoes, tied on her *Kopftuch*, and headed for the river. She made a few little ditches with a stick and watched the puddles drain into rivulets, a simple springtime pleasure she'd always enjoyed. But today it didn't fascinate her, and she tossed the stick on a rock pile and hiked on.

Silently she walked toward the old house site. Too cold to sit on the doorstep rock. Colder than she had expected. With her sweater clutched around her, she walked down the hillside out of the wind and leaned against an elm tree. A tiny smile tugged at the corners of her mouth as she realized where she was standing— right where the old outhouse had stood.

This towering elm had been a mere twig beside the door at first, but by the time they moved to the new house, it was a good-sized tree. Its rough bark bit into her back, but she didn't mind. It was solid, unmovable, something to lean on.

"Oh, for-goodness-sakes, such a silly thought," she muttered. "Leaning on a tree when I should be leaning on God. That's idolatry!"

But God was way up there someplace—far above that blue spot between the clouds—not here, where she could feel His comforting presence.

"Why are you so far away? I need you," she whimpered. Immediately a thought took shape in her mind. *God can't be in the same place as fear. My fear has shut Him out!*

"Oh, Lord, I'm so ashamed! I'm so scared! All I can see is Gertie lying there—like Emmie—like Connie— and Joe standing there with three little ones. Help me let go of it, Father. I want to trust you. Give me something to cling to."

She waited expectantly, but all she could hear was the boisterous river and the wind high in the branches of the budding trees. More desolate than when she had come, she started for home. It was foolish to always expect the answer on the spot.

She wandered along the fence that curved with the contour of the river. At the beginning of the next curve, Papa had buried their stillborn baby. She had been so sick. "We didn't think you'd live," Mrs Geber told her later.

Emma walked on, feeling the spongy wet sod beneath her feet and the sweet spring wind on her face. "I'm here!" she said out loud. "I could have died, and Papa could have been standing there alone with the ten young ones. Oh, Lord, I don't understand why I'm here, and all those other young mothers had to leave their families. All I know is that I trust you. I can take anything, as long as you are with me"

She hurried toward home. Jeanie would be back from school soon.

Emma didn't even realize, till she was coming up the hillside behind the barn, that the horrid knot of fear was gone and she was singing. "Lean-ing, lean-ing. Leaning on the everlasting arms . . ."

She picked up a stick, made a little ditch, and watched a puddle join a tiny stream on its way down to the creek.

Eighteen

More Changes

Emma pretended to be surprised when Carl told her about his wedding plans. "You certainly have my blessing," she assured him.

They would be married in Glenwood City, Olga's birthplace, and planned to live over Len's garage. Emma wasn't happy to hear they had ordered furniture on time payment, but she had to agree that they had no choice.

"I never yearned to be rich," she said, "but at times like these I certainly wish I could help."

Carl laughed. "Oh, we have to have a few hard time stories to tell our kids someday. Don't worry about us."

When Jeanie learned about their marriage, her eyes opened wide. "Miss Harrold will be my aunt? Oh, boy!"

Nora had a reception for the newlyweds, and her mother baked one of her special angel food cakes and circled it with fresh bridal wreath. Jeanie's eyes sparkled as she whispered, "Oh, Mama! I never saw a cake with flowers around it before. Isn't it pretty?"

Ella found a seat next to Emma. "Did you hear? They were married at high noon, June 6. The minister's wife and hired girl were witnesses!"

Gertie laughed. "Can't you hear it some day, when their daughter wants a fancy wedding? They'll tell her about their wedding and remind her that big weddings don't guarantee happy marriages."

In July, Ed came home for a week, bringing the children and his hired girl, Evelyn.

Emma worried aloud to Ella. "She's such a giddy young thing. You don't think Ed. . . ."

Ella laughed. "Oh, Ma, Ed has more sense than that. She's just a hired girl. He can't manage six children alone."

The hectic visit left Emma exhausted, but she was glad they had come so she could see that Ed was in surprisingly good spirits. A few weeks later Ed wrote that Evelyn had run off with a neighbor boy one night. He had found a lady who could stay a few weeks, but he asked for prayers for more permanent help.

That summer Emma received a letter from Mamie. After she read it, she took it to Helen and went back to her room without a word.

Helen usually stood in the doorway and talked, but today she came in and sat down. "I can't imagine what it's like to live in the city and be out of work."

Emma sighed. "They don't even have gardens to depend on. Sounds like both Al and Fred were laid off at the same time, doesn't it?"

Helen nodded. "She did say they expect it to be temporary."

Emma pounded the arm of her rocker with her fist. "Right away, when something like this happens, my mind starts going lickety-split—trying to think of some way to help, or of something they can do to help themselves. It's worry. Plain old worry, that's what it is.

She clasped her hands together and shook them for emphasis. "Got to stop worrying. It's all right to be concerned, but I've got to put them in the Lord's care—pray

His power into their lives, not try to do something myself."

Helen nodded and got up. Words weren't necessary. Emma knew she agreed.

In August Emma and Jeanie stayed a weekend with Carl and Olga. Jeanie thought it was odd to live upstairs, but she liked running up and down the stairs and she admired their new furniture—especially the ivory and green stove and green wicker rocker.

During their stay there was a knock on the door, and there stood Jeanie's dad. The more he apologized for not visiting them, the more uncomfortable Emma felt. At least Jeanie was polite, though she stayed close to Emma.

"She looks so much like Emmie," Ed said, trying to control his emotions.

"Run and see if Olga needs help," Emma told Jeanie.

Ed stood facing a corner, his shoulders heaving. He had just pulled out his handkerchief to blow his nose when Jeanie ran back, saying that Olga didn't need any help.

Red eyed but smiling, Ed asked Jeanie if she'd write a letter to him. "I'll write back," he promised. He pulled out his wallet, handed her a dollar bill, and said, "You go and get a treat before you leave town."

Jeanie was unusually quiet that evening.

"Would have been better if he hadn't come," Emma told Olga. "It only upsets her. He has his own family ."

Joe called a few days later to announce the birth of Donald. Emma was so eager to see Gertie that Roy drove her to Ogema the next day.

"You know how much I wanted a girl," Gertie said. "I couldn't find my voice when they told me it was another boy—but once I saw him, I wouldn't trade him for a million girls. Isn't he cute for a new baby?"

Emma agreed that he certainly was.

"He's so little," Jeanie said on the way home.

"You were that small once," Emma reminded her. As Jeanie chattered on, Emma thought how glad she was that Jeanie was seven. *Eleven more years . . .*

"Got a letter from Mamie and Al today," Emma called Ella to report. "They're coming home! They'll stay with Mamie's folks until they can get their own place again."

"That's great. But what about Fred? Did he find work?"

"Nothing steady, but they've lived there so long he has a better chance of getting odd jobs than Al. I don't know what Al will do here. As soon as I read that letter, I started worrying about how they'll get started here again. Why do I always have to get myself all riled up before I have sense enough to go to the Lord with it?"

"Oh, Ma. It's just human nature to worry."

"You bet it is! And that's no excuse! We don't have to give in to our 'human nature'—we have the Spirit of God in us to help us live the way God wants us to."

"But even St. Paul said the things he wants to do he doesn't do, and the things he doesn't want to do he does. . . ."

"You go get your Bible and read the next chapter! We don't have to live that way. Worry is an awful sin. It's saying, 'God, I don't trust you. I think I can figure out a way to solve this problem.' "

Emma went back to working singing, "Oh, what peace we often forfeit, Oh, what needless pain we bear—all because we do not carry everything to God in prayer."

The potato vines died early that fall, because it was so dry. As always, Emma helped dig potatoes. Hank had come home from the harvest fields and helped, too. Even Jeanie helped, picking the little potatoes that would be cooked in the big black iron kettle for the pigs.

It was backbreaking work, but Emma was thankful for

every last potato. For awhile, when the rain hadn't fallen for days and days, she had feared there wouldn't be any to dig. Suddenly the sky darkened, and here and there the wind spun the dust in little whirlwinds.

Jeanie put her arms over her face and yelled, "Ma! Ma! Hank's throwing stones at me!"

Emma laughed. "No, he isn't! It's hailing!" She ran and put a bushel basket over Jeanie's head. As she held one over her own head and listened to the pelting hail, she chuckled. "How often this child gives us a good laugh when we most need it!"

The carrots and beets were hardly worth digging, and the cabbages were half the usual size, but Emma stored them carefully in the cellar.

As the first day of school approached, Emma talked brightly about how good it would be to see all the children again and about all the new things Jeanie would learn.

Jeanie, usually eager to talk about anything at any time, was silent.

Emma groaned to herself. "Not this again!"

But the first morning, sure enough, Jeanie lost her breakfast. Emma assured her it was only first-day-of-school nervousness—she'd be fine the next day.

Each morning after Jeanie left, Emma sat on her bed and prayed that the Lord would take Jeanie's fear away. By the second week, Jeanie was no longer throwing up. For many mornings Emma sat on the bed and thanked God for bringing Jeanie through that difficult time.

"Lord, you are so wise not to let us see ahead. I wouldn't have the courage to go on, if I could see all the problems that are sure to come up these next eleven years."

That November, though Emma dreaded hunting season as always, she was grateful for the opportunity the men had to get meat for the winter. And the men, though they always loved the sport of it, hunted in earnest this year.

Carl and Len took turns coming down from Phillips to hunt. Esther didn't object to John hunting, because she, too, was glad to get venison.

Only Carl didn't get a buck that season. The deer were hung in the woodshed, and the men would bring them in a quarter at a time for the women to cut into roasts. The scrappy parts they ground into hamburger with a hand-cranked meat grinder.

What would they do without venision? Emma wondered. The tiny cream check barely covered the cost of flour and oatmeal these days.

One day, early in December, Carl and Olga came home. As Emma watched them from the window, she knew something was wrong. They weren't smiling, and Carl had his arm protectively around his wife.

"I should have known it was coming," Carl said, eyes on the floor. "I knew Len was barely making ends meet. With so many people out of work, hardly anyone is buying cars, and most of the time they can't pay for repairs. It sure was tough for him to tell me he had to let me go."

That night Roy, Helen, Carl, and Olga stayed up late talking. The next morning Carl asked, "Ma, it is all right if we move in here with you—use my room upstairs? Roy's willing to have me work with him in the woods this winter."

"Of course it's all right."

"We're hoping by spring we can build a little log house on the forty I own."

"I don't even know where it is. You boys have bought land here and there."

"It's next to Hank and Ella's land, but a quarter of a mile in from the road. There's an old tote road in to it."

Emma took a sip of coffee. "It won't be easy starting

out like that," she said, but the mere mention of a log house had set her pioneer spirit soaring. She stayed awake a long while that night, thinking about what it would be like to start out now, as she and Al had, in a little log house. She also wondered what it would be like to have Olga with her all the time.

They'd piece quilts and crochet rugs and have a cozy winter. Jeanie would love having them home, and Hank, who was working in camp, would only be home weekends.

"At least our furniture is paid for," Carl told Emma a week later, when the last of it was stored in the tool shed. "We'll have something to put in our house when it's built."

They were hardly settled before it was Christmas, and everyone was caught up in a flurry of programs and visiting. Ronnie and Jeanie were about to burst their skins with excitement. They rarely quarreled—just romped and played until they got so wild one of the adults put a stop to it.

Gifts were simple that year, but the family enjoyed just being together.

As Olga and Emma washed dishes one evening, Emma said, "You know, this has been the happiest Christmas we've had for a long while. I forget we're poor."

Olga laughed. "Oh, Gramma, so do I!"

Emma smiled. She pretended not to notice the loving glances Carl and Olga exchanged so often. *Ah, yes*, she thought, as she hung up the dishpan. *Love will soften the hardships ahead of them.*

Nineteen

Another Log Cabin

Emma was glad for more than Olga's pleasant company that winter. She was also a great help with Jeanie, patiently helping her sound out words as she struggled to learn to read.

"I'm no good at it," Emma said with a groan. "Seems like there was always older children to help the younger ones, so I never helped with homework. I'm glad you're here to help."

If there's one thing I'll remember about this winter, Emma thought as she undressed one night, *it will be those two planning that house.* She peeked through the crack in the bedroom door and watched them a moment, heads together, as Carl explained and Olga questioned. Door, windows, roofing, nails, two by fours, chimney brick—so many things they'd need. Where would they get the money?

One evening, as they sat working on their plans, Carl said, "Ma, take a look at this." He slid the paper under the lamp light and pointed with the pencil.

"It'll be sixteen by twenty-four, with the bedroom back here. Think eight feet is wide enough? Want to save all the space possible for the main room."

"Hmm. . . If you turn the bed this way. . . ."

"I was thinking of putting it on an angle," Olga said.

"And here," Carl tapped with the pencil," will be the chimney. And this north window will be the kitchen window."

"Oh, double windows on the south side! That will be nice and light. And the east window in the bedroom—I can just see morning glories peeking in the window."

"We don't plan to do anything with the inside walls yet—just put in a wallboard ceiling and the partition."

"And linoleum, at least on the kitchen side," Olga added. "And of course we don't have to paint the windows right away."

"Close as I can figure," Carl continued, "the door, windows, nails, tar paper for roofing, wallboard, brick and mortar shouldn't run more than a hundred and a quarter."

"You're going to have to sell an awful lot of wood, " Emma said.

A few days later Carl and Roy rattled off to Tomahawk with the old truck loaded with firewood.

"Wish it didn't get dark so early," Emma said that evening as she lit the lamp at five. "Hope they didn't have trouble with that old truck again."

They didn't get home until six thirty, but Olga's eyes glowed when she saw the empty truck.

"You sold the wood."

Carl concentrated on washing his hands. "Yeah. The lady that said she wanted it had already bought some, so we went over to the Maple boardinghouse. Had it almost unloaded—piled for her, too—when she yelled out, 'That's fine, boys! You stop by next week and I'll pay you." He groaned. "Couldn't even buy flour. Just got kerosene and oatmeal."

The next day as she peeled potatoes Olga said, "Gramma, did you have a chimney in your log house, or just the stove pipe?"

"The first summer we only had the stove pipe, but then Al built a chimney."

Olga mentioned it to Carl that evening. "And we don't really need the ceiling or the partition right away either, do we? Or the linoleum?"

"Well . . ." He hugged her. "You don't want to part with that yet!"

"How much would it cost without all that?"

Carl scribbled a few minutes. "Maybe we could get by for about sixty bucks."

When they came home from hauling wood the next week, Carl shook his head. "The lady at the Maple still couldn't pay. One of the new customers said her son brought her a load, so the other one took it all—but we had to let it go for a buck and a half a cord."

"Did she pay you?" Olga asked, holding her breath.

Carl nodded. "Hadda buy flour and gas. Ain't much left."

Olga was her usual cheerful self the following week, but Emma often saw her staring out the window. Meanwhile, Roy and Carl got up at five each morning, did chores, ate breakfast, grabbed their lunches that the women had tied up in a dish towel, harnessed the horses, and took off for the woods back of Carl's property.

This winter they were cutting spruce for pulpwood that would be sold to the paper mill and cutting dead tamarack for firewood. As they worked, Carl selected tamarack logs for the house.

When Emma tucked Jeanie into bed one evening, Jeanie said in a pensive little voice, "I wish I had lotsa money."

Emma sat down on the edge of the bed. "Now just what would you do with 'lotsa money'?"

"I'd give it to Carl and Olga for their house."

"That's just how I feel, *Liebchen*. I don't mind having them here—and you don't either—but they should have their own home."

"But where are they gonna get the money?"

"I don't know—but I know who does know! Want to ask Him for it?"

Jeanie squeezed her eyes shut and folded her hands. "Father God, if you want Carl and Olga to have a house all by themselves, you gotta help 'em get some more money. They need a whole lot more. Please show 'em where to get it. Amen."

"Goodnight, *Liebchen*. They'll get it. You'll see!"

By the middle of February Emma didn't have to light the lamp until almost six. "So good to see the days getting longer," she said.

"Is it ever!" Olga agreed, smiling broadly.

What, Emma wondered, was making her so especially happy today? She hadn't stared out the window once.

After supper dishes were done, Olga disappeared upstairs and came down with an envelope. As Carl dried his hands she hugged it to her, smiling up at him, and said, "Wait'll you see what I found!"

Emma stifled her curiosity as they sat, heads together, reading pages of fine print. Eventually Carl sat back, fingers laced across his chest, and said, "Hate to do it, but it is a solution." He turned to Emma. "Ma, we've found a way we could get the money. We could surrender Olga's life insurance policy."

The next day Olga wrote the letter, and the waiting began. Meanwhile, a letter came from Ed. "Well, for-goodness-sakes," Emma exclaimed. "Listen to this!":

Dear Mother and all,

I know this will be a surprise, but I'm getting married in a couple weeks. Her name is Peggy, and her husband died several years ago. She's had an awful time trying to manage with four little ones. I've known her since we've been in Eau Galle and always admired her, and I guess she feels the same about me. She's a jolly person, hardworking, and I've never heard her complain. You'll like her.

Her oldest daughter, Rosemary, is two years older than Allison, Gordon is a little younger than Shirley, and then come Frank and Kathleen. It won't be easy to put these two families together, but it can't be any harder than it's been trying to take care of them alone. We admit that we aren't madly in love with each other, like we were with our first spouses, but we're certainly attracted to each other and we're excited about this new challenge. We ask for your prayers and your blessing.

Love to all,

Ed

Emma put the letter down, pushed up her glasses, and dried her eyes on her apron. "I'm glad," she said.

Carl shook his head. "Whew! Ten kids!"

By midwinter, with many of the cows standing dry, income was at an all-time low. The long fingers of the depression had reached out to the most remote parts of the country. But when Emma saw the pictures of the soup lines in the cities, her heart ached and she felt wealthy by comparison. They had a home, wood for heat, venison in the woodshed, eggs from the chickens, vegetables in the cellar, and always enough milk.

It was only when her stockings could be darned no more, and Jeanie outgrew her overshoes, that she felt the need for money. The stocking problem was easy to solve—she simply cut off the feet and sewed the ends shut. The overshoe problem was a bit more complicated. Emma knitted heavy homespun socks for Jeanie to wear in the overshoes instead of her shoes, and had her carry her shoes to school in a bag.

The one thing Emma missed was coffee. The barley "coffee" she roasted in the oven with a little molasses was barely tolerable. Jeanie gagged from the smell.

The last week in March, Carl said, "Well, we got all the logs hauled out for the house—even a few for a barn. We beat that spring thaw."

"Now, if only the money would come," Olga said

with a sigh. The first week in April Carl leveled off the site. Still no check from the insurance company.

The day before Easter, Emma came back from the separator room with a pitcher of milk. "The men didn't buy any Easter egg dye," she told Olga. " They got some jelly beans and a few chocolate covered marshmallow eggs, but none of the larger candy eggs. Why don't I boil the eggs with onion skins? At least they'll be yellow, then, instead of white."

"And tonight we can decorate them with crayons," Olga added.

Jeanie was delighted next morning with the hand decorated eggs in Emma's little brown basket. She and Jeanie and Hank rode to church in Carl's little blue Whippet, bumping all over the road to avoid sink holes.

Helen was no longer the only woman on the men's side—Olga sat with Carl, too. Emma was glad that Rev. Krause didn't show any objection.

There were no new Easter bonnets this year. Probably not a new item of clothing in the whole congregation, unless it was a pair of badly needed shoes.

"Jesus imparted His righteousness to you," Rev. Krause proclaimed. "When we come to the Father in prayer, He doesn't see us in our sinfulness. He sees us covered with Jesus' robe of righteousness."

Emma closed her eyes. Yes! She could see that glowing robe covering her, making her acceptable to the Father. Oh, she'd remember that when she felt too unworthy to come to the Father in prayer.

Jeanie's legs were—swinging—swinging. Emma laid her hand on Jeanie's knees, and they became quiet.

"All because of His glorious resurrection . . ."

Now Jeanie was tying to touch the pew ahead with her toes. "Sit still!" Emma whispered. *Little ones never used to bother me like this.*

The organ began playing, "I know that my Redeemer

lives." Emma smiled down at Jeanie, singing at the top of her high little voice. A thrill of joy flowed through Emma, but it wasn't because of the music. It was knowing the He was alive! *Soon we'll be with Him forever and ever!*

The day after Easter, Olga came in from the mailbox waving a long envelope. "Finally!" she said breathlessly, taking the scissors and cutting open the envelope. She fished out the check. "Fifty-eight dollars and sixty-five cents! Oh, Gram, I can't wait till Carl gets home!"

A building bee was arranged for Saturday. "No women or kids," Carl ordered. "You'd just be in the way. Pack us lunches, and we'll cook our own coffee."

It was so late when Carl and Roy got home that day, they did chores first and then ate supper.

"Even got the roofing on," Carl said. "I've got a lot of chinking to do yet, but it's actually up! Henry and Roy hewed the logs smooth on the inside as we laid each row. That's almost a lost art—there aren't many left who know how to use a broadaxe. Al was busy helping me with details, and of course Floyd helped a lot. I never coulda done it alone."

"Oh, I don't know about that," Olga said, "but it would have taken a lot longer. When can we move in?"

Carl shrugged. "Depends on the weather and what Roy and I have to do around here this week. Gotta lay the floor and plaster the cracks on the outside." Carl worked long hours that week.

On Friday night he said, "I was thinking, if you women wanna come and see the house tomorrow—"

"When we gonna get there?" Jeanie asked each time they rounded another curve in the old tote road, and the house still wasn't in view.

Olga laughed. "I think they took the path of least resistance when they made this road."

"That they did," Emma agreed. "They knew it would

only be used to tote supplies to camp, so they weren't about to cut big trees or move boulders."

"I see the house!" Jeanie yelled, taking off like a cotton-tail.

"Doesn't it look big? We'll have lots of room," Olga said, as they walked in and picked their way around tools.

Emma didn't answer, but she was thinking that it wouldn't seem so big once all the furniture was in, the partition built, and the ceiling completed.

"I like the smell of new wood," she said. "And look at those south windows! You tell me what house plants you'd like, and I'll start some for you"

They ate lunch sitting on the floor boards with their feet dangling down into the crawl space below. Only a few more boards and the floor would be done.

"Hope these boards don't shrink," Carl said. "If they aren't dry enough, we'll sure have cracks between the boards."

Olga laughed. "I could sweep the dirt through the cracks. Wouldn't have to use a dustpan."

"Mama" Jeanie called from the east end of the house. "Look here!"

"Looks like an old wood-chuck hole to me," Emma said. Jeanie giggled, and Emma followed her eyes to the bedroom window and through. She saw Carl and Olga's silhouette as they embraced in the doorway.

"What's so funny?" said Emma. "One of these days you'll be in love!"

"Oh, Mama! I will not" Jeanie insisted.

When May came, Emma stood by the east window and watched the rusty old truck chug down the driveway loaded with Carl and Olga's furniture.

"Silly old fool" she muttered, blinking back tears. "They won't even be two miles away."

A dozen times that day she caught herself turning to

tell Olga something. At supper time, Jeanie picked at her food and said, "I wish they coulda stayed here. It was more fun."

Carl came to get water every day. On Thursday he poked his head into Emma's room and said, "Olga said I should ask if you want to come over Saturday."

Emma laughed. "You won't have to ask us twice! Jeanie's been pestering to go over all week."

"Oh, it's nice and cozy," Emma exclaimed, when she stood in the doorway Saturday forenoon. "And the new wood smells so fresh. And my goodness! All the color!"

Her eyes roved from the green checked table cloth to the cream and green stove, and, to her right, to the green wicker rocker, the multicolored rag rug, the shiny walnut table with the silver candy dish in the middle—a wedding gift from Nels and Minnie. And all around, through the windows, fast-greening grass and bushes.

It was certainly different form her own first log home. *No wonder we women liked houseplants, rag rugs, and patch-work quilts. Everything else was black or gray or brown. And we only had little bitty windows, so we couldn't even see much of the outdoor color.*

"Dinner's almost ready," Olga said as she drained potatoes. "Jeanie, wash your hands, and you can put the silverwear around."

Jeanie poured a dipper of water into the white enameled washbasin on a shelf next to the stove, and Emma added a splash of hot water from the teakettle.

Olga lifted the lid of the ice compartment of the little brown icebox and took out a loaf of bread. "See my bread box?"

Emma peered into its towel-lined depths. "Why, that's a good idea."

"And down here," Olga continued as she opened the icebox door, "I have room for all my spices, jelly, syrup, and things."

She saw Emma looking at the array of china and cookwear on the shelves to the right of the door. "Gertie says she has some green and white checked gingham I can have to make curtains. And Carl's going to make shelves over there for books and things." She pointed to the corner to the left of the door. "By fall we'll have the bedroom partition in and the ceiling."

Jeanie bounced on her toes. "Oh, it's just like playing house!"

Olga smiled. "Well . . . almost."

After dinner they went to see the little log barn Carl was building for the cow and heifer Roy had given him.

Jeanie ran to the little out-house. When she came out she said, "How come there's only one hole?"

Emma chuckled. "We had a two-holer because there were fifteen of us using it! It'll take a few years before Carl and Olga need a two-holer!"

Carl was showing Emma where he planned to grub in potatoes around some stumps when they heard a car bumping along through the brush.

The whole family piled out of Geeorge and Sadie's little black Ford. The older children dragged out a big box and set it down in front of Olga.

"It's your housewarming present," Dorothy said. The older children grinned and the little ones giggled.

Cautiously, Olga lifted the flap. Out popped a brown chicken's head. *Cluck, cluck, cluck!*

"A chicken," Jeanie squealed.

"A cluck!" Glen informed her.

George lifted the cluck out, and the girls took out chick after chick after chick. "Eleven of 'em," said Glen.

"They're beautiful!" Olga exclaimed, as the cluck waddled off down the path with her little ones peeping along behind her. "Thank you so much!"

The next day Emma reported to Minnie, "You should have seen all those beaming little faces. They were so happy to be able to give something.

Twenty

Scrimping and Saving

All winter, whenever Hank had been home, Emma endured the radio for hours after she went to bed, grateful that it didn't keep Jeanie awake. Sometimes she fell asleep out of sheer exhaustion, but other nights the radio's squealing and crackling tormented her hours on end.

During the spring she had tried to ignore it, thinking she could put up with it until Hank went out west. Then, shortly after Carl and Olga moved, he announced he was staying home this summer to pitch for the Rib Lake baseball team.

At first Emma was happy for him. Then she remembered that all the games were played on Sundays—Hank would never get to church—and the team was sponsored primarily by tavern owners. When she expressed her concern that he would be led far from God, Hank's response was a disgusted snort.

"Oh, Ma! That's ridiculous," he snapped, and punctuated it with a slammed door.

Emma saw her prayer-work laid out for her.

When Hank turned on the radio that evening, the prospect of hearing it night after night overwhelmed her.

"Oh, Lord," she pleaded into her pillow, "help me!"

She needed her sleep, didn't she? How could Hank be so inconsiderate? Finally she slept, embroiled in troubled dreams, and woke with a headache.

For two more nights she struggled. "Lord, I don't understand," she wailed beneath the covers. "I'm so tired. Why don't you help me?"

The thought came: *Remember your love-pattern?*

Oh. I haven't thought of it for a long time. Love is gentle, long suffering, not easily provoked, thinks no evil. . . .

"Lord, I'm sorry for those thoughts and for my impatience and my self-centered thinking and for not even thinking about Hank. I should be glad he's right here at home. Forgive me!"

She rested a bit in a wave of peace, but the radio's noise was as loud as ever. "Lord, I'm still angry at Hank. But I don't want to feel this way. You'll have to change my feelings"

Ever so gently and imperceptibly, the ugliness drifted away and she slept.

The next night Emma stretched out in bed, expecting the Lord's sweet peace to envelope her. Instead the announcer's staccato shouts pelted her ears.

"Oh, no!" she groaned. "Not a prize fight!" She let out a little sob of frustration. She didn't feel like thinking about that pattern. She wanted to go out there and rail, "What's the matter with you! I've got to get some sleep one of these nights!" But she knew he'd defy her. Maybe even slam out of the house to a tavern.

Gentle . . . kind . . . long suffering . . . not easily provoked.

When she woke the next morning, she realized she had drifted off to sleep while pondering her pattern.

Emma watched Jeanie skip rope on the hard-packed red clay driveway—shiny brown hair bouncing, counting breathlessly. On and on she skipped until she missed.

"Rats!" she exclaimed.

Emma was about to scold her for her unlady-like remark, but she bit her tongue. *Let her act like an eight-year-old*, she reminded herself. All too soon she'd be a self-conscious teenager.

Emma laid her knitting down and called to Jeanie, "Come here a minute. I've got an idea."

With her rope swinging in wild circles over her head, Jeanie ran to the porch and plopped down on the swing.

"I was thinking—Carl won't be using his room anymore. How would you like to have it?"

Evening was the wrong time to tell Jeanie something that stimulating, Emma realized, as she prattled on and on after bedtime.

At breakfast Emma said, "Now, before you start moving things up there, we'll clean it real good. We'll take the bedding out on the line, scrub the floor and woodwork, and wash the window and the curtains."

Jeanie was already thumping up the stairs yelling, "I'll get the quilts down."

Amazing, Emma thought hours later, *how much help Jeanie can be—when she wants to*. Usually she grumbled and griped her way through her Saturday chores, but today she had run up and down the stairs fetching broom, dustpan, water without complaint.

"Every Saturday you'll clean it," Emma instructed, "and if you want it to look nice, you'll always hang up your clothes."

When the white iron bedframe was washed and the bedding brought in from the line, Emma brought up her best sheets and pillow cases and a pink bedspread Jeanie's dad had given her for Christmas years before.

Jeanie smoothed its geometric design. "Oh, Mama! It's so pretty! Can I have Grace and Ruby come and stay overnight?"

Emma nodded. "One at a time, though."

Emma felt a little lonely sleeping alone that night, but it was comfortable without that little wiggle-worm next to her. During the coldest weather, she'd have Jeanie come down and sleep with her again.

By July the lawn was brown, except for the shady spots under the box elder trees. When Emma washed clothes she carried every bit of rinse water to the tomato plants and the few petunias that still bravely bloomed. The hoped-for raspberries thrived only around brush piles and in partial shade, but one week Carl and Olga picked enough to sell a few quarts in Tomahawk.

The following week Emma and Jeanie helped pick, too, and went along toTomahawk.

At the crest of every hill, Carl shifted into neutral and coasted until the car nearly stopped while they guessed, using trees and posts as markers, how far the car would go before he had to put it in gear again. "Someday, when we don't have to be so careful about using gas," he said over his shoulder to Emma, "I'll probably still coast down every hill—I'm so used to it."

At the A&P store, Emma carefully counted her money. It would be nice to have a box of corn flakes or some soda crackers, but she decided she'd rather spend the twenty cents on ice cream cones. They made the cones last almost to Spirit Falls.

That night, after Jeanie was in bed, Emma had a long talk with the Lord. "Father, I wish I could earn some money—sell something like the woman in Proverbs. I want to be a help to Roy and Helen and especially to Carl and Olga.

"I'm so proud of them, the way they laugh and have such a good time even when they don't know where the next sack of flour is coming from. Never hear them complain. I know you're going to bless them for that. I think you enjoy watching them, too, clearing that land

and taking such good care of their little farm. They're being faithful with what they have, just like you taught, Jesus.

"I want to be faithful with what you've given me, too. Show me what I can do to be a blessing to my family and neighbors."

Emma waited and waited for the Lord to put some idea in her mind, but she went to sleep without a new thought.

The next morning discouraging thoughts dragged her spirit down like a sinker on a fishing line. How foolish to think that she, a fast-aging woman, could be an asset to her family. She'd be more and more dependent, not more helpful. At least she could take care of herself and Jeanie—and Hank, when he was home. That was something.

She was sorting the raspberries she and Jeanie had picked in Zielkies' woods when Carl suddenly appeared in the doorway, wanting to know if he could build a few shelves in the cellar for Olga's canned goods.

Emma didn't see any reason why he couldn't. There was certainly plenty of room. As he talked about tomatoes and string beans, Emma stared at his ragged overalls. They had been patched and patched again, but still there were new holes. Carl had never been one to be careful. If his pants caught on barbed wire, he was more likely to keep going straight through than back up and unhook them.

Wonder if Olga has denim for patches, she thought after Carl had left. She'd hunt in her rag box and see what she would find. Better yet, she'd offer to come over and do some patching. That was something she could do—and darn socks, too! She'd been helping the other girls for years and had never thought of it being of much value—but wasn't preserving as good as earning? *After all*, she reminded herself, *a penny saved is a penny earned*.

"Well, Ma," Ella said one fall day as they pared apples on Ella's back porch. "You going to stick with Hoover?"

Emma sighed. "I haven't made up my mind. Poor Hoover didn't put that chicken in every pot, much less a car in every garage. But then, we can't blame the President for everything. I don't know . . . maybe the Democrats should have a chance."

"Seems like people are ready for a change," Ella agreed.

In November, when Roosevelt was elected, Emma felt a surge of hope and determined to pray faithfully for him.

"If people would pray as much as they criticize," she said sternly to the menfolk as they sat arguing politics one Sunday afternoon, "our country wouldn't be in such trouble!"

One morning early in December, after Roy had given Emma her third of the cream check, Emma sat down at Helen's kitchen table.

"I don't know what to do. You know how much it means to Jeanie to have a new dress for Christmas. She's been looking at material for weeks—has a green tweed picked out. But she needs stockings and underwear, and there just isn't enough money. . . ."

Helen poured coffee and sat down. "We'll think of something. Maybe we can make something over."

Emma shook her head. "I thought of that. I don't have a thing that would work."

"Maybe I have." Helen went upstairs and came down with a bright green wool flannel dress. "I haven't worn this for years. It may have a couple moth holes."

That afternoon Helen ripped and Emma sponged and pressed the pieces. They agreed to wait until an order came from Sears Roebuck and then put it in one of the bags.

Emma folded the pieces with the largest ones to the

outside. "I can cut it when she's in school. She'll never know it wasn't new!"

When the order came Emma put the material in a Sears bag and piled it with the other items.

"Oh, goodie! The order came!" Jeanie squealed when she ran in after school. "Oh! My material!" She pulled it part way out of the bag, while Emma held her breath. "It's 'sposed to have little colored spots!"

"They must have had to substitute," Emma hedged, but before Emma could stop her, Jeanie had pulled the material out of the bag and begun to unfold it.

"It's all pieces!" she wailed.

Carefully, Emma helped her pick up the pieces. "Come here," she said patting the edge of the bed. "I know you're disappointed. We thought we could fool you. There just isn't enough money for new material."

"But where did it come from?"

"It's a dress of Helen's. We ripped it apart."

"Helen gave *me* her dress?"

Emma nodded.

Jeanie grabbed the material, hugged it to her, and ran to find Helen. She came back a few minutes later, eyes shining. "Oh, Mama! Wasn't that nice of her! It's gonna be so pretty!"

When the women spoke to each other later, after Jeanie was in bed, Helen laughed. "Isn't that something! We thought we'd fool her, but she turned around and fooled us!"

Emma went back to her rooms smiling, but for another reason. As Helen stood sideways in the pantry doorway, Emma had noticed that there'd be another baby in the spring.

TwentyOne

New Worries

There would be three more grandchildren in spring, Emma soon learned. George dropped by to say he and Sadie expected another baby, and soon afterward Ed wrote that he and Peggy would have a special first anniversary gift.

"Lord," Emma whispered as she lay down for a nap. "I know children are a blessing. But George and Sadie aren't well, with his bad heart and her goiter. And Ed and Peggy have had so little time to get settled with their two families. But you know best."

She woke startled, and sat on the edge of the bed a few moments to sort out reality.

"Oh, dear," she chuckled. "I'm glad *that* was a dream." She had dreamed she was carrying another baby. She had even felt it kick. Amazing how vivid a dream could be.

"Father," she prayed as she pulled on the heels of her slippers, "make the new little ones a blessing."

She got out her quilt patches and glanced at the clock. In only two hours Jeanie would be home. She wished she didn't dread the evenings, but it was so nerve wracking to try to understand all her jabbering—and how that child could jabber!

That evening Jeanie didn't even have her coat off when she started chattering. She pulled a piece of neatly folded yellow tablet paper out of her reading book and handed it to Emma.

Dear Mother,

You are invited to attend a party for George Washington's birthday on Wednesday, February 22 at 2:00 p.m. There will be entertainment and refreshments.

Miss Hinkie and pupils of Liberty School

"Well, now, that's real nice!"

Jeanie hopped up and down in front of her. "You'll come?"

"I don't see why not."

Jeanie rattled on and on, while Emma thought about calling Ella. Maybe they could go together.

Tuesday evening Jeanie came home, excited as usual. "Where's the cookies? What kind did you make?"

"Cookies?"

"For the party tomorrow!"

Emma frowned. "What are you talking about?"

"You said you'd bake cookies for the party!"

"I did not!"

Jeanie was near tears. "You did, too!"

"Now don't you get sassy, young lady. I don't know a thing about cookies."

Jeanie began to cry. "I asked you, and you said 'Uh huh.'"

"Oh-my-goodness." Emma sat down in the rocker. "I'll bake some in the morning."

Jeanie wiped tears on her sleeve. "We're 'sposed to bring 'em in the morning, so we can have everything ready when the mothers come."

Emma put her arm around Jeanie. "I think it will be all right if I bring them when I come."

It was fun to see all the eager little faces and to watch the proud young mothers, but with all the little siblings fussing around and the school children talking and laughing, Emma didn't get much out of the little program they had prepared. She wondered if anyone noticed that she was trying to laugh when the others did.

After Jeanie was in bed, Emma sat thinking long after her usual bedtime. No use denying it. She was losing her hearing. Just a couple weeks ago she had been surprised when Al and Mamie came over on a Sunday afternoon. When Mamie saw her surprise, she said, "I told you we were planning to come over when we were going down the church steps this morning. Guess you didn't hear me."

Good thing Reverend Krause had a good, strong voice. Emma sat near the front, and that helped, too.

But the worst part was trying to understand Jeanie. Emma sighed as she took out her hair pins. Wasn't it hard enough taking care of a young one at her age? Now this yet!

A few days later she was rocking and knitting and thinking, when suddenly Carl stood in front of her.

He apologized when he saw how startled she was. "I thought you heard me come in."

"Guess I was deep in thought," she explained.

When he left, she thought, *Why did I say that? Why can't I admit I can't hear?* In bed that night she realized why. She was scared.

One morning Emma saw Helen go to answer the phone. Little Ronnie ran in and sat down with her in the rocker. He loved to hear her sing little German songs and, of course, have a ride on her foot. Emma looked up and saw Helen standing in the doorway, smiling and watching them. In a few minutes Ronnie scampered off, and Emma went back to darning socks.

A while later Helen appeared at the doorway again.

"Look at this," she said, pointing to the corner of the room where she kept her sewing cabinet. "Why didn't you watch him?"

Puzzled, Emma followed her. What a mess! Tangled thread, needles, pins, binding, ribbon were all over the floor.

Emma shook her head. "You asked me to watch him?"

"I stood right there at that door," Helen yelled, "and told you Carl had called and I had to go down to the barn to tell Roy something."

"Oh-my-goodness—I didn't hear you!" Emma bent down and began to pick up spools.

"Oh, never mind that," Helen said, quietly. "I was so scared! He could have got at the stove—knives—anything."

Emma's knees were still trembling when she sat down again. "That does it," she told herself. "I've got to let people know I can't hear."

When she told Ella about her loss of hearing, Ella wasn't surprised at all. "Oh, Ma, we've been noticing it for a long while. We try to be sure we have your attention when we talk to you, but sometimes we don't realize that you haven't heard us when you smile and nod and say, 'Uh huh'. You're just going to have to tell us when you don't understand us."

They talked about the possiblity of her getting a hearing aid, but Emma was set against it. She had seen the trouble her sister Winnie had with hers. Wasn't worth the money.

Before she had time to think more about her hearing loss, her body gave her a new concern. One day, early in March, she carried in an armload of wood and let it roll into the wood box. As she straightened up, a pain shot around her rib cage and over her right shoulder. She stood still a moment before she took off her coat and overshoes, but as soon as she moved and breathed, back it came.

Emma eased herself into the rocker. Could it be her heart? No—she'd heard somewhere that heart attack pain was on the left side. She relaxed a bit; it did feel better when she sat very still.

Her next task was to fill the water pail. Though she pumped with her left hand, the pain shot over her shoulder again. She was glad Helen wasn't around to hear her gasp.

"Oh, Lord! Help me get through this evening," she prayed.

Fortunately, Jeanie was too interested in a new library book to even notice that Emma winced as she heated left-overs for their supper. All she needed was a good night's sleep, and she'd be fine. No one would have to know.

But when she got up to put wood in the stove before bed, Helen and Roy heard her groan.

Roy stuck his head in the doorway. "Ma! What's wrong?"

He helped her to her rocker, and Helen tucked a quilt around her shivering body. Emma managed to tell them where the pain was and when it had started. Tears of dismay and fear spilled down her cheeks as Roy went to call the doctor.

What was happening? This awful clutching pain—could it be a heart attack? Jeanie would be so frightened! And Helen's baby was due soon. She had to be well.

"Doc's delivering a baby in Town-of-Hill," Roy reported. "He'll come as soon as he can."

She could hear the fire snapping now and then and the rocker creaking whenever Roy moved. Some blessing she'd be, sick like this. *Father, please take this pain away!*

Roy put wood in the stoves and offered her a drink of water.

Finally Dr. McKinnon arrived and listened to her chest.

"Pleurisy", he announced. "It's an inflamation of the lining between the lung and the chest wall." He grinned.

"Bet you thought you were having a heart attack."

Emma smiled weakly.

He patted her hand. "Your heart's fine. I'm going to put a tight binder on you, so you can't breath deep, and I want you to stay in bed at least a week. Longer, if you still have pain."

It was past midnight when they got to bed. Emma wanted to tell Roy and Helen how sorry she was to be such trouble.

"Shhh," Roy said. "Don't try to talk. I know you don't want to be sick." He helped her to bed. "You try to sleep now."

In the morning Jeanie tip-toed in, dressed for school. She tried to smile. "Helen says—oh, Mama!" She crumpled beside the bed and sobbed into Emma's pillow.

"There, there, *Liebchen*. I'll be fine"

"I don't wanna go to school."

"You go. I'll be fine. I just have to rest."

Days blurred together. Olga came, and Ella and Gertie and Mamie, but Emma couldn't talk. She couldn't tell them how she feared for Jeanie. Her little face had lost all its color, and her eyes had dark circles under them. Emma knew she wasn't eating. Every morning she begged to stay home, and every night she sat in the rocker—rocking, rocking.

A week later, Emma was sitting up when Clara came. "The pain's not bad anymore," she assured her.

"I'll only stay a little while. Don't try to talk," Clara said, pulling a chair close to Emma.

Emma clung to Clara's hand. "I'm so worried about Jeanie. What would happen to that child if—if—" Emma blinked back tears.

"Emma, Emma! Aren't you the one who's always telling us it's a sin to worry?"

The next morning she took the binder off. It felt good to draw a deep breath again. In another week the pain was entirely gone. Hank came home and carried wood and water, and Olga helped with the washing. Jeanie's cheeks glowed pink again.

In April, the three new grandchildren arrived within a week of one another: all girls. Ed wrote of Ruth's arival, and George reported that his new daughter's name was Gardia.

A few days later, Roy poked his head into Emma's doorway to say that the doctor and Helen's mother were on the way. Before noon, little Marilyn had arrived. Emma thought Marilyn an especially pretty baby, but Hank just mumbled that all newborns looked alike.

One evening, as Emma knitted and Hank read the paper, Jeanie asked, "How do mothers know they're going to have a baby?"

Emma gulped. "Uh . . . well . . . the doctor tells them."

"Oh. But when they get fat, they know. That's why Helen was so fat. The baby was in her tummy, huh."

Hank put down the paper. "It was! Why, I thought the doctor brought them in his little black bag."

Emma shook her fist at him over Jeanie's head, and he hid his taunting grin behind the paper.

When no more questions came, Emma let her breath out real slow. Oh, dear! Something else she hadn't thought about having to deal with!

In June Ed wrote and said if someone would bring Emma and Jeanie for a week's visit, he would take them home. Carl and Olga said were glad to go.

"I'm like a little kid," Emma said as they rode along. "I can't wait to meet Peggy and the children."

"That's got to be it," Olga said, as they hunted for Ed and Peggy's house. "There are kids all over the place!"

Emma certainly did like Peggy. Her round face with its wide smile had a charm all its own, and Emma didn't even think of comparing her with Connie. Emma soon felt like they had known each other for years.

While they were cutting up potatoes one afternoon, Peggy paused and rested her hands on the edge of the huge kettle. "Grandma, is it a lot different rearing Jeanie than it was your other children?"

"Oh, I should say it is," Emma said. "Sometimes I think it's been harder than all the other thirteen put together."

"Do you think it's the times we live in?"

Emma sighed. "I suppose that's part of it. Seems like Jeanie is always wanting something we can't afford or wanting to do something I don't know anything about. When my children were small, they just went along with the older ones. I didn't have to make all those decisions."

"But isn't there a different sense of responsibility, too?"

"Yes, there is. It's sort of like having someone look over your shoulder while you work."

Peggy sighed. "That's the way I feel about Ed's children. Every time I have to decide something, I wonder what Connie would have done. Do you think I'll always feel like that?"

"Oh, I don't think so. After all, you've only had them a year, you know. Another thing you must remember is that love grows. Don't feel guilty if you don't feel love for Ed's children like your own yet."

Peggy's face flushed. "I needed to hear that. Sometimes I feel so guilty."

"Don't you worry! Get to know them, and you'll love them."

"I'm trying. It isn't easy. But, Grandma, Ed is such a good husband and father." She put the potatoes on to boil. "The only time I've really been angry with him was last fall, when he took the older children to the fair and spent almost as much as a week's groceries."

They were both laughing when Ed came in. "Aren't you two talked out yet?"

Peggy smiled up at him. "Oh, goodness no! I think they should stay another week."

"How about it, Ma?"

Emma shook her head. "I'd like to. I'm having such a nice time, and I know Jeanie is, too. But I can't expect Helen to water my garden forever. If we don't get rain, I'll lose the few vegetables I've been pampering."

Ed's four oldest children went along when he took Emma and Jeanie home. Ordinarily, Emma would have enjoyed the ride, but watching nothing but brown, bone-dry grass made her heart ache.

"At least we'll have potatoes," she said. "Roy has worked so hard irrigating the potato field. Doesn't that sound odd—irrigating in our part of the country? You remember the field across the river?"

Ed nodded.

"Well, I don't know if Roy was planning for another dry year when he planted potatoes there this spring, but it sure has worked out well. He borrowed a hydraulic ram from Oscar Norlin and built a little dam and ran pipes over into the field. Water runs day and night! Roy keeps changing the hose, and the whole field gets watered. Isn't that something?"

"Sounds like a great idea. Good thing the river hasn't gone dry. It must be awfully low."

Emma was near tears when she saw her garden. In spite of Helen's watering, the tomato plants were curled and dry, and there were only a few little misshapen green tomatoes on the vines. The beans were completely brown, and the cucumber leaves looked as though boiling water had been poured on them. *Well*, Emma consoled herself, *at least we'll have potatoes!*

TwentyTwo

Fire!

One evening in September, Jeanie ran in after school yelling, "Mama! You oughta see the smoke—way down near Tomahawk."

"Smoke?"

"Uh huh!" she panted. "The woods is on fire."

"Oh, dear . . . as dry as things are. . . ."

They walked up to the maple hill where they could see smoke rolling up perhaps twenty miles away.

Emma's stomach felt sick. What, other than hard rain, would prevent it from raging right on through to the dense timber to the south and the stands of evergreens around homesteads, right to where they stood. The dry fields wouldn't be a barrier.

"Mama? Will it keep coming?"

"Oh, it's a long way off," Emma said. "We'll pray for rain—lots of rain."

When Emma helped Roy with the milking, she asked him what he had heard.

"Mailman says there's a rumor that resort owners were back-firing, trying to protect their property in case of fire, and it got away from them."

"Such carelessness! Usually when anyone backfires, they have a big enough crew to put the fire out as soon as it burns over a little patch."

"Wind coulda turned and they weren't prepared. That can happen easy."

The next day Emma was curious enough to walk up the hill again. There was even more smoke in that area and in several new areas as well.

Roy said it looked really serious and there were some ugly stories going around that fires were being set on purpose, so men could get a few days' work.

"Oh-my-goodness! Could people be that desperate?"

"Well, the state pays twenty cents an hour."

Emma wiped her face with her apron. "Who ever thought it would come to somthing like this?"

Day after day the smoke rolled, and more and more men went to fight fires.

"If you want to go," Emma told Roy, "I can manage the milking."

The next noon he sat down at Emma's table. "I'm gonna have to go and help, Ma. You sure the milking won't be too much for you?"

"I can do it. Don't you worry."

"I'll get home when I can, but the governor has sent the commander of the National Guard to help protect the New Wood timber. He's bringing a couple hundred CCC boys with him.

Carl and and I are supposed to blaze a trail for them as close to the fire as we can get, without getting surrounded, and they'll follow with a crawler tractor and a two-way plow. The CCC boys will patrol that line and put out fires when sparks fly over. Pretty sure we can save the timber that way."

Emma bit her lip. "Oh, be careful!" she pleaded. "And don't worry about us. We'll be fine here."

Several anxious days passed.

Roy got home to sleep a few hours each night and helped some with chores; then off he'd go again.

The fire was halted at that line, and the CCC boys were sent back to camp. The timber was saved.

"But it's not over," Roy said wearily, as he sat on the porch swing, hand over his burning eyes. "The wind's straight out of the east. We're going to have to stop it at the county line. Farmers from all the townships around are gonna help. At the rate it's traveling, we've got a few hours yet. Gotta get some sleep."

He insisted on helping Emma with the milking in the morning, and then took off with his water tank and a shovel.

"I hate to hang the diapers out," Helen said as she put them through the wringer. "Everything smells smoke."

Emma scanned the sky. "I keep hoping to see rain clouds, but it's only smoke. Did you see how red the sun was yesterday evening?"

She peered into the two barrels of water standing by the house—and up at the ladder leaning against the house. She couldn't imagine either herself or Helen trying to put out fires way up on the roof. And what would happen if sparks fell on the barn roof? All those old, dry shingles! And the evergreen trees out in front! If they caught on fire, the heat would be unbearable and surely the house would go.

She walked back to her rooms, praying, "Father, I don't know when I've felt more helpless. You are our only help."

She sat down with her Bible and opened it to the Psalms. "God is our refuge and strength, a very present help in trouble. Therefore I will not fear, though the earth be moved, and though the mountains be carried into the midst of the sea. . . .:

Though the evergreens catch fire and the house burn and the barn go up in flames, still will I trust thee, Emma paraphrased. *Oh, Lord, I don't feel that trusting. Where would we go? What would we do?*

She paged through and read: "I will say of the Lord,

He is my refuge and my fortress; my God; in him will I trust. . . . There shall no evil befall thee, neither shall any plague come nigh thy dwelling."

I don't know how you're going to do it, Lord, but you will protect us.

She started when George walked in.

"Roy said to stop by and tell you they expect the fire to hit the county line early this afternoon. Colonel Heinz is there. The National Guard Commander left him to help us. We wanna back-fire, but he says he won't allow it. 'Too many fires set already,' he says." George picked up the dipper and took a long drink of water. "We've got a lotta guys with water tanks, but I don't know what's gonna happen when it hits that stand of pine and balsam down by YY and 86."

Emma groaned. "Those poor farmers down there."

"They're plowing furrows around the buildings and watering down roofs." He shook his head. "I gotta get going."

The cows wandered home at five, and Emma began milking and wishing Jeanie would stop following her around asking questions. "Are they going to put the fire out? The big boys say all our houses and barns are gonna burn, and we'll have to move way far away."

"Oh, they don't know what they're talking about! It isn't going to get past the county line. Go give the chickens some water."

"I hear a car!" Jeanie yelled and ran to see who it was.

She was back in a few minutes. "Mama! Carl and Roy came home, and they're lyin' on the lawn."

"Lying on the lawn?"

She nodded. "They've got their faces right down in the grass."

Emma's heart did a flip when she saw them. Their eyes! She brought them wet wash cloths.

Carl rested a while and then went home, his eyes almost swollen shut.

"Did they say anything?" she asked Helen.

"They couldn't hold it at the county line road," she answered. "They had to back-fire at the next road. If the wind doesn't change—"

She turned away, and Emma went to take off her barn jacket pleading, "Father, help us!"

Roy was still lying on the lawn when she went to bed. She hoped he was sleeping.

When she got up about midnight and looked out the window, Roy was gone. She hurried to the kitchen window. The car was there. He must be up in bed. She stepped out on the well platform to see the glow of the fire, now less than three miles away.

Murky, smoke-laden air hid the stars, but she could make out the outline of the weathervane on the barn. Could it be? Yes! The wind had changed! It was coming from the south, not the east.

"Oh Father, thank you! Thank you!" The fire would turn to the already burned-over area and there, fuel-starved, it would end.

Eventually Emma slept, but she woke early and peered out the east window as the sun's first rays cut low across the lawn. The grass was sparkling! It looked like it had rained!

She ran out barefoot. Yes! Yes! The grass was full of little droplets. There hadn't been rain, or even dew, for weeks and weeks. Why, even the driveway looked damp! There must have been a light rain!

A few moments later, his eyes puffy and red, Roy shared her elation and quickly drove off to see what had happened. He was back in a half hour. The fire was under control. The wind had driven much of it to the bunned-over area, and the light rain had prevented its spread over the damp fields.

Later Roy told them more details of the battle at the county line. His eyes were still blood-shot, and he kept them closed as he talked.

"There musta been at least a hunderd men down at the county line yesterday morning. We wanted to back-fire, but Colonel Heinz wouldn't let us. We figured if it hit that stand of evergreens, there'd be no stopping it, but he wouldn't listen to us." Roy stopped and took a sip of coffee. "When we got down there that morning, we could feel hot wind 'blowing from the northeast but we couldn't see flames—just smoke, smoke, smoke.

Sparks started to fly, and we kept putting 'em out and soaked each other down, and all of a sudden it was like those trees exploded. There was a draft strong enough to pull our hats off. Man! The heat! I remember hearin' a roar, and Carl and me dived into the ditch face down, but the others ran across the road and kept going."

He shook his head. "Thought we were done-for. Didn't think anything could get that hot. When it got quiet, we got up and saw it had gone right over us. There were burning things that looked like catalog pages on fire, flyin' through the air. The field across the road was catchin' fire. We ran with our tanks and started put-tin' out fires, and some of the guys came runnin' back to help."

Jeanie interrupted. "What were the burning things flying through the air?"

Roy chuckled. "Rutabaga leaves! Finn John had a patch along the road. The heat dried out those big leaves, and they came flying through the air in flames."

"Did you get it out there?" Emma asked.

"Well, Carl and me could hardly see, so the Colonel sent us home. We'd been out there days before most of the guys. When we left, we really didn't know what was going to happen. We just couldn't go any more. We fig-ured as soon as we got a little rest, we'd plow furrows around the buildings."

Emma gasped. "You mean—you really thought it might keep comin' right through?"

Roy nodded. "If that wind hadn't changed and we

hadn't got that light rain. . . ."

Emma didn't hear the rest of the conversation. Deep in her heart she was thanking the Lord over and over and over.

The following Saturday, Jeanie ran out to play after dinner, but bounced back in yelling, "It's raining! It's raining!"

Emma dropped the dishtowel and bustled out on the porch. "Oh, Lord, thank you!" she whispered when she saw the quarter-sized drops on the steps.

She joined Helen and Roy and little Marilyn on the porch swing, as Ronnie and Jeanie ran in wild circles on the lawn, squealing and yelling.

"Rain, rain, don't go away!" Jeanie hollered up at the sky.

"I haven't got the heart to call her in," Emma said. "It's warm enough for them to run it in, isn't it?"

Roy grinned. "Let 'em run."

It was pouring now, and Jeanie and Ronnie held their faces up and caught rain drops in their mouths, then shook their heads and ran some more.

A cool breeze swept across the porch, and Emma called, "Jeanie, you come in now! It's getting chilly."

It took several calls before Ronnie and Jeanie stood dripping on the porch. Little Marilyn waved her arms and laughed.

Emma hustled Jeanie into dry clothes. "Don't think you're going to run in the rain every time," she warned. "This was a special occasion."

TwentyThree

Blessings Untold

If Jeanie was aware of Olga's expected baby, she didn't say anything to Emma. But when she came home from school December nineteenth, and Emma told her Carl and Olga had a little Albert, she didn't act as surprised as Emma thought she'd be. But she certainly was delighted. She wanted to go and see him right away.

"Tomorrow," Emma said. She didn't tell her it had been a long, hard labor, and little Olga was exhausted.

My goodness . . . Carl, a father, Emma mused as she got ready for bed that night. Only twelve when Papa died, and now a fine young man.

The yearning to talk to Papa—to tell him all about the fire, the boys' narrow escape, Ed's new family—so much more—welled up in her and came out in a sob. "Jesus! Please tell him for me."

"I think those chickens are laying all those eggs because they know how much you need them," Emma said with a twinkle in her eye. Olga had brought in seven eggs one February afternoon when Emma spent the day with her—patching and darning.

Olga hung her wool plaid jacket on a hook by the door. "Only two days this month that they haven't each laid an egg."

Six of the eleven chicks George and Sadie had given them had been pullets. One little rooster had met an untimely end under the cow's foot, three others had provided Sunday dinners, and one still strutted and crowed in the little log barn.

"Bet you thought I wasn't ever coming in," Olga said. "When the baby's alone in the house, I hurry to get back, but today I did things I've been putting off for weeks."

"Oh, I remember that feeling so well—working with my heart in my throat when the little ones were alone in the house. Those years Papa worked in camp, I had to feed the stock, and I just couldn't take the little ones out with me in storms and cold. For a long while I was so scared. . . . It's a long story—sometime I'll tell you—but I had to learn to trust God to take care of them. I couldn't do it alone."

Emma held the needle up to the light, threaded it, and continued. "I didn't know it at the time, but this was my schooling in learning to trust. Wasn't long before Al was big enough to be out on his own—coulda fallen in the river, or out of a tree, or got trampled by a horse." She waved her hand. "And that was only the beginning. One after the other, they grew up and started driving cars and traipsing all over the country."

Little Albert started to cry, and Olga picked him up and held himclose. "In other words, we can't keep them safe. We have to trust God to take care of them."

Emma smiled and nodded. "I never did learn that lesson good as I should—always have to drag my thoughts back by the nape of the neck when something new comes up."

Olga laughed. "And that's pretty often with Jeanie, huh?"

"Oh, yes! I never know what's next. Don't know if it's

keeping me young or sending me to my grave a little quicker."

Olga patted Emma's shoulder. "It's keeping you young! Believe me!"

"Mama, a man came to school today from Phillips to check on the practice teacher," Jeanie announced one afternoon. At recess he came up to me and said, 'Little girl, I just found out who you are.' He put his finger under my chin so I hadda look at him, and he said, 'I hope you grow up to be like your mother. She was a very special person.' He had tears in his eyes."

"Do you know his name?"

"Mr. Milne—something like that."

Emma nodded. "He was the principal when your mother went to teacher's training school. They called it Normal School. She often spoke of how kind he was." What a good feeling, to know that Emmie was still remembered after ten years.

In April Ella's daughter Myrtle had to have her appendix removed. Ella stayed with her in the Marshfield hospital for several days, and when she got home she called Emma.

"Ma, Jeanie's dad is in that hospital. He's dying, Ma."

"Oh-my-goodness. He wrote at Christmas time that he had been in bed a good share of the year, but I didn't know—"

"He wants to see Jeanie."

"Oh, dear."

"Ma, it's awful. He has tumors on his back, and he's not even in a regular bed—it's an ugly contraption."

"Poor man! But I can't let Jeanie see that. She gets upset so easy."

"I tried to tell him that. He just cried."

In early May, the call came. Ed was dead.

Ella and Gertie rode to the funeral with Roy, Emma,

and Jeanie. They went to Ed's house before the funeral, where the body lay in the living room. His little son and daughter, too young to realize what had happened, played happily outside.

Amanda, Ed's wife, was cordial to them all. Much as she'd miss him, he had suffered so terribly she wouldn't wish him back.

Jeanie stood at the casket, teary-eyed but not grief-stricken. She had hardly known her father.

In church Emma realized it was May 10—exactly ten years since Emmie's death. Had Emmie lived, she realized, *she* would be sitting there in black—a widow at twenty-nine.

Emma had always wondered what had become of Emmie's bedroom furniture and cedar chest. She had bought the ivory set while she was teaching school. She hesitated to talk about it now, but it was her only opportunity. When she had a moment to speak to Amanda quietly, she asked if Jeanie could have Emmie's things. Amanda said they could come and get them any time.

Jeanie was quiet on the way home, but she didn't appear to be disturbed. That night, after Emma was in bed, she felt a little hand on her shoulder.

"Mama? I keep seein' him lyin' there."

"You want to sleep with me tonight?"

She crawled over Emma, cuddled close, and slept.

Several weeks later Len got a trailer and hauled Emmie's furniture down from Phillips. When it was set up in Jeanie's room, she dragged everyone one who set foot in the house up to see the bed with the curved footboard and the vanity dresser with hinged mirrors—and the cedar chest.

While Jeanie floated high on her cloud of elation, Emma battled engulfing waves of grief. Seeing the furniture had brought tears to Emma's eyes, but she wasn't prepared for the emotion that swept over her when they went through the cedar chest.

Ed had saved all the linens with Emmie's handwork on them and several of her dresses. Jeanie listened and questioned as long as Emma was willing to talk about Emmie. In a small candy box they found a tiny crocheted "bowl."

"What is it, Mama?" Jenaie asked, spinning it on her finger. There was still thread attached.

Emma took a folded magazine page from the box and unfolded it. "Oh!" Jeanie exclaimed. "A baby cap!"

Emma tried to smile. "She was making it for you."

Tenderly Jeanie laid it back in the box and then threw herself into Emma's lap sobbing, "I wish I coulda known her!"

Emma patted her head. "You will, *Liebchen*, you will."

That summer, instead of glowering at gloomy skies, Emma gloried in them. Rain was still welcome, although the lawn was greener than usual in July. More important, the pasture and hay fields were green, and one could almost watch the corn grow. Did God ever tire of hearing her say thank you?

One August day Emma watched Jeanie trudge up the hill on her way to spend a day at Olga's—again—with a twinge of jealousy. Jeanie was often discontent at home, always wanting to do something that required more of Emma's patience than she could spare.

Emma shook her head and began to clear the table. How did Olga put up with her? The other day Jeanie had dropped all the freshly-washed diapers in the dirt on the way to the washline. Another time she had let Jeanie use a whole cup of sugar to make fudge and showed her how to hold it over the water pail to cool while she beat it. When Jeanie beat it and beat it, and it didn't get thick, Olga realized she was letting water splash in the pan and back it went to boil and boil again.

But Emma could understand why Jeanie was drawn

to Olga. She had a way of making everyday activities special. She'd say, "After dinner we'll put a blanket out in the shade and shell peas," or "When Little Albert wakes up, we'll take a walk in the woods."

When Carl brought Jeanie home that evening, she raced in yelling, "Mama? Do you have an extra needle? Olga was helping me sew a doll dress, and I was threading the needle and it fell right down the crack in the floor." She made a dramatic gesture and sighed. "It was her last needle!"

Emma rummaged in her sewing cabinet and found a pack of needles. She stuck three of them in a piece of cloth and handed it to Carl.

He grinned. "Thanks, Ma. Dreamed the other night that the cracks were so wide in that floor, I had to jump from one board to another."

Emma laughed. "Oh, dear! If you had to jump, imagine what little Olga would have to do!"

"Thought that lumber was dry, but it just keeps shrinking."

"Would be nice if you could get linoleum for that kitchen end."

"Well, if enough people die . . ." he said, with a twinkle in his eye.

"How you talk!" she chided, as he grinned at her over his shoulder on his way out the door.

Carl's grave-digging job had certainly been a blessing.

Olga said once, "We start wondering where the next sack of flour is coming from, and then somebody dies and Carl gets three dollars for digging the grave. Oh, I don't mean I'm glad when someone dies—but I can't help but be grateful for the money."

The last week in August, Emma told Ella, "I'll walk over one day this week. I know how much work you have before your anniversary party. I can help you with some mending and give the girls a chance to be together before school starts."

"What on earth do you kids find to do in that woods all the time?" Emma asked Jeanie, as they walked up the last hill toward Ella's.

"Lotsa things. We swing on saplings and we explore and build houses and play hide-'n-go-seek. Can I run ahead?"

Emma smiled as she watched Jeanie's little legs fly along. Such energy! The hill seemed unusually steep today.

Emma stopped, only vaguely aware of her pulse pounding in her ears, and smiled up at the neat white house and big red barn as she thought of those nine busy lives. So much to be thankfur for—hay in the mow, sileage in the silo, oats in the bin, and plenty of potatoes.

"Lord, I'm so content I could cry. I can walk these two miles—don't even have to ask anyone to drive me. I can do my own housework, take care of Jeanie, and even help with milking and go mend for the girls. And that special peace you give me! You're all I need! Oh, Jesus," she whispered, eyes closed now. "You are here—in me, around me...I can't explain it. I'm ready to come to you anytime. Don't even think of it as dying—just walking into your world, like walking through a doorway.

"But, Lord," a sob came out, "I want all my children to know you like this. It hurts so much when they won't listen—when they think if they give their whole lives to you, that you'll take all the fun out of it. They just don't know that fun is nothing, compared to the joy you give. Father, if I long to have them know you and love and trust you, how much more you must long for that!"

She looked up and saw Jeanie waving to her from the driveway, but she couldn't hear what she was calling to her.

"I'm coming," she called, and began walking.

She blew her nose and dried her tears. Ella wouldn't understand—not yet.

Excitement bubbled up in her as she thought about

the anniversary party. Twenty-five years. She could see Henry and Ella and their seven children lining up for pictures, all smiles. Seemed like yesterday that Ella was a young girl working beside her.

"Whatever would I have done without her," she said to herself, and began to sing softly as she walked. "Shall we gather at the riv-er, that beautiful, beautiful riv-er. Gather with the saints at the riv-er that flows by the throne of God. . . ."

TwentyFour

A Job to Do

The morning of the anniversary party, Emma immediately thanked God for a clear day, though she had spent a restless night. She tried to think of what she had eaten the day before that might have upset her, but couldn't recall anything unusual.

She drank tea instead of barley coffee that morning, nibbled a little toast, and decided that physical discomfort would not rob her of this exciting day any more than she would have allowed it to rob her twenty-five years ago, when the house teemed with wedding guests. If Papa could only see Ella now—a fine woman, a beloved mother.

"I'll be careful what I eat," Emma reminded herself as they drove in the driveway and up the hill.

So many dear ones she saw all too seldom. Len and Nora. John and Esther. Clara and Walter. So many more. She forgot all about not feeling well.

Although the food looked delicious, Emma decided to wait until others were served before she ate. She found a quiet corner in the living room—nearly everyone was outside—and tried to ignore the tight feeling across her chest and the twinges of pain. Surely she wasn't getting pleurisy again. She'd never had it in warm weather.

She was in line to get some food when she noticed that the forks were almost gone, and slipped into the kitchen to get some more.

Jeanie dashed in, laughing so hard she could hardly talk. "Oh, Mama! You shoulda heard—"

Emma didn't hear anymore. An invisible vise had clamped her chest in a crushing pain.

"Go . . . play," she gasped and staggered toward Ella's bedroom. If only she could make it to the bed. She heard Jeanie scream, and arms and voices were everywhere.

"Don't lay her down. You could kill her!"

"Someone! Get more pillows!"

"Call the doctor."

"You'll be all right, Emma."

"Don't struggle, Ma," Roy urged.

She caught a glimpse of Jeanie's wide-eyed horror. She couldn't talk, but her mind was pleading, pleading, "Oh, Lord! Not yet! Not yet! She needs me!"

The pain was everywhere—her arm, her shoulder, even her jaw. And that terrible crushing weight on her chest.

Someone spoke the words she already knew: heart attack.

Faces . . . voices. "Breathe deep! Relax!"

Would it ever end? If it weren't for Jeanie, she'd so gladly let go.

"Can't reach Dr. McKinnon," she heard.

"Dr. Baker from Rib Lake is coming."

Where was Jeanie? Was she all right? She tried to ask, but she couldn't get the words out.

Pain. Pain. Hard to breathe. So many people . . . *Lord, help me!*

"The doctor's here."

Hands opening her dress, gentle hands moving a stethoscope over her chest. A shot in her arm.

The vise releasing, releasing. She was drifting . . . drifting.

Dark. Quiet. "Ella?"

"I'm here, Ma."

"I'm so sor-r-y."

"Don't you worry. You're more important than any old party. Here, drink a little of this."

"So tired."

"Ella?"

"No, Emma. It's Clara. Just rest."

"What time is it?"

"Almost five."

"Supper time?"

"No. Five in the morning."

"Oh, dear. You should be home in bed!"

"Take a little drink of water."

Emma turned her head away. Hadn't better drink. Would have to use the bedpan. Afraid to move.

"Are you in pain, Emma?"

She nodded and struggled to speak. "My little girl. What would she do? I'm all she has."

Clara squeezed Emma's hand. "No, Emma. Who does she really belong to?"

Tired . . . so tired. Pain. Clara's words slipping past her.

Daylight. Footsteps. Doors closing.

"Mama?" Jeanie beside the bed. Ella coaxing her out.

Poor baby! What will she do?

Faces at the doorway. Roy, Helen. Carl, Olga. Hank, chin quivering. Al, Mamie. All so quiet—patting her hand, leaving quickly.

I must be dying. My little girl! What will happen? Clara. What did Clara say? Have to remember. . . .

Night again. Lamp casting gnome-like shadows on the wall.

Ella's soft hand smoothing her brow. Poor Ella. Must be so tired.

Daylight.

Jeanie's stricken little face. Must try to smile—tell her to go to school. Pain!

Quiet. Alone. *Lord, I don't understand. I'm all she has! No . . . Clara.said, "Who does she really belong to?" I see. She belongs to you, Lord! You will take care of her.*

So tired. Hard to breathe. Want to sleep and sleep. *Jesus, I'd like to come to you—be with you all the time—feel that wonderful feeling, like I felt up in the woods, all the time.*

"Ma, try to drink a little tea."

She turned her head away again.

Roy's voice now. "Ma. You drink this! We can't do it for you!"

She took a few sips.

Night. The shadows again. The smell of the kerosene lamp.

Drifting . . . drifting. Walking in a flower-strewn meadow. Beautiful! Papa's strong arm around her. Happy! So much to tell him! *There must have been a million times I wanted to tell you something, but you weren't there!*

Emmie—running toward them!

"Ma! Please take a drink."

Tears. "I want to talk to Emmie!"

Ella's voice shook. "Did you forget? Emmie's gone!"

"I know. I mean when I get there."

Daylight. Jeanie holding her hand in both of hers. "Mama? You better?"

Smile. Nod.

"Ma, we've been trying to get Dr. McKinnon. Talked to him on the phone. He says to lie still—but you must drink. He'll come soon as he can."

Ella, always fussing. Pulling sheets. Washing her.

"Leave me alone!"

"I'm sorry, Ma. I have to."

"What day is it?"

"Tuesday."

"Ella, I want to tell you something. I'm not afraid to die."

"I know."

Quiet. Alone. Can see that terrified little face. *Father, take care of her.* Tears running down. Too tired to wipe them.

That odor—disinfectant—Dr. McKinnon!

"Well, let's see what goes on here!" His voice bounced off the walls of the little room. "Sit up a bit now. Breathe through open mouth. Again. Again. Pain?"

"Uh huh."

"Hard to breathe?"

"Uh huh."

"It will take awhile, but you'll be all right."

Emma's eyes flew open. "I'm not going to die?"

His laugh boomed. "Not now, you aren't!" He patted her hand. "A blood clot's shut off the circulation to part of your heart, but it will heal. Other blood vessels will take over in time."

"They will? What should I do?"

"I'll tell your daughter. You mind her. Got to get you back on your feet." He smiled at Jeanie, hovering by the doorway. "You've got an important job to do."

Alone again. *I'm not going to die. I'll move. I'll walk. Oh, but I don't feel like struggling!* Tears again. *I wanted to be with Papa—to talk with Emmie.*

Night again. Pain still there.

"Ma, here's some farina. Will you eat a little?"

Too tired. Want to sleep. Dream of Papa—Emmie.

"Mama? Aunt Ella's cryin' cause you won't eat."

"Tell her I'll try."

Someone always trying to get her to drink, eat.

Night again. Restless. Right leg cramping.

"Ma! What is it?"

"Leg cramp."

"Swing your legs out! Here! Sit up."

"Ahh. It's going away. I'm sorry."

"You just call! Don't try to sit up alone."

Days blur together. So many faces. So many questions. "How are you? Still have pain? You want some water?"

Morning.

"Ma, Clara's going to stay right by you while you sit in the chair, and I'll change the bed."

"Glad to sit up. My back aches."

"Take it slow! There now. Dizzy?"

"A little."

Good to be back in bed again.

Jeanie—sobbing quietly beside the bed.

"There, there, *Liebchen*. I'm going to get well. The doctor said so."

Little arms hugging her—choking her. "Oh, Mama!"

Don't know how I'll ever walk again. Got to try.

Evening again. "Ma, I'm going to help you sit up in the chair again. Maybe your legs won't cramp tonight."

Her left leg cramped once, but she didn't groan—just swung her legs out and sat up—by herself. Emma smiled when she lay back down. Big accomplishment!

The next day she sat up three times and walked a few steps, feet feeling full of pins and needles.

Each day a little more. Out to the living room. The next day to the kitchen rocker. So weak—but better. Much better.

Days long now. Things had been going too well! How could life change so fast?

Tired of lying. If only she could move that little piece of paper over the door—just a bit so it would match the next one. Moved it, mentally, a thousand times. Got to look at seams that do match. I shouldn't always look for what's wrong.

Jeanie—pale and hollow-eyed—often sitting quietly beside her, stroking her hair. "You're better every day, Mama."

Got to try to walk alone. Have to walk alone before I can go home.

"Ma! What are you doing?" Ella yelled, dropping a plate in the dishpan.

"Got to start walking on my own." She sat in the kitchen rocker a while and said, "Guess I'll go back to bed now."

Ella rushed to her side. "Remember how I used to dream of being a nurse?"

"Uh huh."

"I still like taking care of people—but I don't like having them sick."

"You're real good at it. Real good."

That night she dreamed of Papa and Emmie again. So good to be with them. But it was only a dream.

In a few more days she was able to sit up half an hour without feeling dizzy. There wasn't much pain anymore.

Time to go home. Would be good to sleep in her own bed again. Would be good to sit in her rocker and look at Papa's picture and Emmie's. Would have to do just a little at a time, and let Helen help her.

"Mama? You sleepin'?"

"No. I was thinking. I think we should go home. Will you help me?"

"Oh, Mama! I'll carry water and wood, and I can cook some."

"Go get Aunt Ella."

"You're so weak yet," Ella said. "You know you can stay here as long as you want to."

"I know. But I want to go home. You've been so good." She couldn't say any more.

The next day Roy came and got her. He parked as

close to the house as he could, and she walked in, leaning on his arm all the way to her rocker.

Jeanie ran back to the car to get another load.

Emma looked up at Papa's picture and over at Emmie's and sighed. "Not yet," she whispered. "Not yet. I've got a job to finish here first."